HELL AND ITS PLEASURES

LUCIEN BURR

HELL AND ITS PLEASURES
Lucien Burr

Cover Art by 4RESNA

Book Design by Lucien Burr

Ebook design by Lucien Burr

Category (Adult Erotic Fiction)
Genre (Paranormal/ Romance / LGBT)

PROLOGUE

'Depart from me, you who are cursed, into the eternal fire prepared for the devil and his angels. – Matthew 25:41

"The mind is its own place, and in itself can make a heaven of hell, a hell of heaven." – The character of Satan, in John Milton's *Paradise Lost*

For most of us sinners, Hell remains a concept out of reach; human fear that has been pulled taught and tormented or hope that is singed away by years of agonising over goodness, properness, primness. For some, a serenity is found in this quiet but painful limbo. They can live with the threat of Hell and be comforted by the promise of Heaven. Peace comes to them in waves, and they may live a life in the quiet of the Lord's whisper, where He soothes their worries and ensures they are safe. His children.

These are the people who believe they are inherently good. Inherently righteous.

But what of those of us who stray from God's light? What of those of us sinners who turn our backs with glee?

What about me, Alessandro, a don whose life had been given to the Lord in earnest—but whose pleasures and hopes and desires were never snuffed out by the Lord. Not once. Not once ever satiated.

What about me, who has tasted Hell on his tongue? Who would welcome it again? Who covets it; who would make a covenant with a Prince of Hell to live my days in that fiery torment?

Well, I shall tell you: there is no salvation for me except what I find in the 'now'. If I have forsaken my eternal life at God's side—a life of nothingness and internal peace, in exchange for the bliss of a body torn asunder by demonic desire—then there is nothing more for me here.

I knew it as soon as Asmodeus returned to its domain and left me in its wake, quaking in rapturous bliss, aware of my own mortality and the years I had wasted being good and pure. I regretted never letting myself partake in human pleasure. I regretted piety, for all it had stopped me from feeling.

I will walk into Hell with my eyes on God and let the demons take me from behind.

ONE

It took two weeks for the bishop to arrive.

I'd seen Bishop Fazio from afar on the day of his appointment to our little town, just hours after Bishop Jonah was buried. Since then, he had changed very little. Around him wafted an air of disapproval like incense, which clouded him in a constant haze. His resting expression had been permanently altered by the persistence of this feeling in his life, and his brows ow barely eluded his eyelashes, so low they clung to his face. He *had* aged remarkably poorly, however, which I chose to believe was down to his bitterness. He had a great size to his pot belly, but he wore it somehow gracefully, walking with an ease and a comfort I found hard to emulate. His priestly garb fitted him the way mine never had: like a second skin. Like it was meant to be there.

I disliked that I felt anything close to jealousy for him in that moment. Seeing him arrive reminded me that I wasn't intending to stay here. Priestly duties would be nothing but a distant memory if I got what I wanted.

Yet I still felt anxious.

I was giving up the mortal plane, was I not? My body, as it

was, meant nothing to me. Here, on earth, I felt pathetic, worthless—but beneath Asmodeus' lustful gaze, purpose burned to life in me. Worth was bestowed upon my body.

It had given me a use. What was more, I had the good fortune of feeling that purpose truly when I was touched. Pleasure and pain and every thrust had been a grounding motion, as if for years my soul had wandered above my head and now was being stuffed back inside. I felt myself as I never had before. With Asmodeus, I felt *good*.

In this way, I managed to conquer my fears about Bishop Fazio's visit fairly easily. I had burned anything that might have led to conclusions I wanted no-one to reach: anything ruined by the demon's touch or cum had burned away the same night I replaced the summoning scroll in its restricted cabinet.

The first night, I had been anxious. He would know—Bishop Fazio would sniff me out, smell the sulphur on me, know intrinsically what I'd allowed to be done to my body. But over those two weeks of waiting for him to take the time to visit our small town, my fear became blunted.

He stood now in the abbey's courtyard, which was little more than a beautiful strip of grass and potted plants against the sandstone exterior. The ocean moved in the distance, a faint blue ripple near the horizon. Bishop Fazio stared out at it, hands clasped around his back, and a rosary was threaded through his fingers and around his wrists like manacles. His fingers stroked over the cross solemnly, or perhaps sensually. His manservant—a miserable looking child—announced my arrival and deposited me like that, standing in the courtyard with nothing more than the Bishop's summons to understand the situation.

Bishop Fazio did not turn around. I tried to breathe deeply and slowly, hoping the steadiness would ease the anxiety that had flared to life in my chest. The voice of Bishop Jonah, the old man who had confirmed me, whispered the knowledge of my blasphemy to me as the silence stretched. *He knows. He knows, he knows, he knows all about you, you filthy whore. He knows how pathetic you look with a cock in your mouth, how your eyes light up when you are on your knees in worship to a demon: knows the stark contrast with which you have worshipped our Lord. You are seen and you are known and you are found filthy.*

And Asmodeus' voice in my ears, its deep chuckle resonant as it saw me, and lauded me for that same filth: *Little priest, you are the most willing piece of meat I've ever fucked.*

Bishop Fazio twitched and my mind went suddenly blank as I chased all impure thoughts away, as if he could tell what was in my head. He looked over his shoulder—but not at me. As my heartrate softened, I heard how the grass crunched underfoot, and saw the child had returned with another priest in tow.

Oliviero.

"Bishop Fazio," Oliviero said sweetly. I realised belatedly I hadn't acknowledged the Bishop, and certainly not given him his dues. I bowed with Oliviero now and went to kiss his ring. One after the other Oliviero and my lips skirted over a gold signet ring glinting on the Bishop's finger. The sea breeze tousled through our hair; my mind corrupted the moment. I saw briefly Oliviero and mine own mouth pressed against the Bishop's cock, lips parting in desperate adoration—

Stop it.

I felt the flush consume my cheeks and bowed lower, but the Bishop caught my expression. A finger grazed beneath my chin and he raised my face upwards. If he had pressed firmly, he might have felt the last remains of the scab from Asmodeus' more brutal touches. I noted his fingers carefully avoided the slow healing cuts across my right cheek where the demon had pressed its clawed fingers into the giving flesh; the first time it had split me open. Bishop Fazio's eyes scanned my face. I felt exposed, in a way; worried God would show him my secrets, that he would see every humiliating desire I had pulsing in my veins. But from the way the bishop looked at me—all pitying, lip-curling disgust—he thought very little of me. Certainly, I thought he had not even considered a man like me might have summoned Asmodeus to our realm.

"Don Alessandro," Bishop Jonah said. His voice had an airy pitch to it, as if only half his lungs were in working order at any given time. A wheeze accompanied every sentence, and so he blew my name and title out in rasp that did nothing to dissuade me of the certainty I, and most priests of my station, disgusted him. He was much closer to God than I was by the church's standards. He must have thought so, too.

"You are the Lord's humble servant. You have reformed yourself in His light; I have heard the tale of what you encountered in the scribe's room, and I shudder to think of that unholy presence intruding on sacred ground. But faith won out. Faith won out."

He repeated that line and shook my own head for me. I went limp with the touch, whorish for anybody, and vaguely remembered to close my eyes as if in thoughtful prayer lest they roll back into my skull.

I was let go, and I drooped forward. I splayed my hands on the warm grass and tried to feel below, for the depths of a plane I had never seen but had been conditioned to believe in. Of course, it wasn't heaven I prayed to. I prayed to it. To Asmodeus. I tried to feel him waiting for me in Hell.

Prince, why have you left me here? Give me the strength to crawl to you. I will drag my body through Hell for you to touch me again.

Bishop Fazio's wheezing rattle of a voice cut over the prayer. I flinched at the sound and rocked back onto my haunches, standing with a crack and a groan and all my wasted time flaying the flesh of my heart.

The bishop looked between us. "Tell it to me, as you remember it. The both of you."

I looked over to Oliviero, frightened. How *did* the young man remember things? Had weeks softened the image of the demon, and me before it? Or had he ruminated on it, prayed on it, cultivated a truth more damning even than my reality?

He saw me looking and flushed. "Please," he said. "It is your story to tell. I merely. . .found you at the right time."

"God found me at the right time," I said quickly, and the bishop let out a thoughtful humming noise. His arms moved as no doubt behind his back he continued fondling that rosary.

I did not say aloud what I was really thinking: of the new religion I had given myself to. I tried to inhabit the fearful, religious part of myself, trying to understand what that version of Alessandro would say. I summoned both false outrage and false fear.

Shaking my head with falsified revulsion, I muttered, "It looked. . .like a distended, larger human, though it had horns, a tail, and claws. Its skin was reddish. And its eyes,"—I saw them in my mind's eye, the way it looked at me, and I felt fire burning in my groin—"Uh, it, uh. . .It seemed confined to the circle. When Oliviero so bravely disturbed it. . ."

"It was my duty," Oliviero whispered, and he made the sign of the cross with a furtive prayer accompanying the flight of his fingers.

I glanced up at Bishop Fazio, whose gaze hadn't moved from me.

"The circle," the bishop wheezed. When our eyes met, he recoiled ever so slightly and turned his eyes back to the horizon; back to God's holy light. "How do you suppose it got there?"

This felt like a question for me. Oliviero stilled by my side as if he had never considered that before now. I felt the distance between us grow, and spiritually I was stranded on my own isle, moored and alone. My fingernails dug into the soft flesh of my palm, and I focused on the bite of them against my skin. Pain had an anchoring force to it. I let it pull me into its harbour, breathing through the sting.

"My holy bishop," I said. I cast a look back at Oliviero, whose head had fallen deeper in his prayer, and I said, "I would like to speak with you alone."

Why I did this, I couldn't tell you. I had opened my mouth to say one thing—a bland lie about finding the circle like that, about wandering in during the dead of night by chance—and said instead something that frightened me.

The bishop turned around bodily now. His eyes drifted over me, over Oliviero, and then to the child servant, who had been so unmoving since delivering my holy brother that I'd forgotten he was there.

"Child." Bishop Fazio summoned the boy forward with one hand. "Have young Oliviero show you the abbey's chapel. Both of you shall pray for God to have mercy on all of us sinners."

The boy and Oliviero dipped their heads and bodies lower and turned so hastily I thought them to be fleeing. What had I done? My stomach twisted—foolish as I was, I hadn't thought I would be my own demise.

A lie, Alessandro. You were willing for all your brethren to hear you scream that night the demon took you. You knew this was coming. You knew you would be caught, and you still wanted it.

"Speak, Don."

Unease shuddered out with my exhale. I shuffled forward and placed my hands over the sandstone wall so I might extract the warmth from the stone, and not because I wanted to hold on to something with dear life.

I took a few moments and the bishop let me. I closed my

eyes and breathed deep, and in some mockery of every time I had prayed for God's intervention in the years before now, my desperation was answered. From the soles of my feet, heat seeped up into my body. I could feel every inch of my flesh come alive, every vein popping with the warmth, and when it reached my head, I shuddered. I heard no voice, and saw no sign, but I felt it—I felt Asmodeus. I felt a calling, a claim on my soul and my body, and the urge to get onto my knees to dig my own grave, my own path to Hell, became almost unbearable.

I imagined burrowing into the earth. I imagined dirt in my lungs turning muddy with the wetness of my frantic breaths. I imagined entombing myself in my urge to reach Hell. If I could only get lower. If I could only—

"Don Alessandro?"

I jerked back to this moment and shook my head. The motion did little to clear my body of the sensation. My cock twitched, a bodily reaction to a presence only I could feel. I pressed myself closer to the wall and I leaned into both the stone and the surety I had of some greater force on my side.

"I. . .am worried about the circle," I told him. Rather, I opened my mouth, and let something speak through me. It was. . .not possession. It couldn't be, by the church's definition, and as much as I might have wished it, Asmodeus had well and truly been sent back to its domain. This was—

Inspiration.

"What worries me greatly, Bishop, is the knowledge that something of that design could not appear miraculously. God would not allow it."

The bishop sighed but did not interject. I continued, "The abbey must have been infiltrated. Someone must have. . ."

I trailed off and the bishop came beside me, sniffing and groaning as he adjusted himself. He clasped his hands over the walls with the rosary between his fingers. The wind picked up and went through my hair and that rosary, sent them straining in the air, breeze whistling as it tried to drag us both out to sea.

"You are simply too good of a man to speak the truth," the bishop said. He would not look at me as he said it. "But you know as well as I that no one except your confirmed brethren would have access to that room. Let alone the scroll."

I felt a terrified flush beginning in my cheeks and tried to shield it by dropping my head into my hands, fingers tousled and gripping my own hair. The bishop made a noise with his teeth and sighed.

"I know. It is horrible to believe. But. . .it is the only truth I can think of."

I let the question hang. What were we meant to do? What was *I* meant to do? I had a horrible vision of the bishop's next words. *We will remove such illicit material from the abbey.* Or: *we will reinforce access to those tomes, we will find a way to protect them from dirty, unclean hands.*

If it was my idea, then I could get close. I could see what other illicit books we had stored in that section. Though from what I recalled, nothing as evil as what I needed was stored here.

At least one of us would know.

I put a shake into my voice, placed a finger at my quivering lip, and whispered, "Are there. . .worse things than that tome in this abbey, Bishop Fazio?"

He looked at me strangely, and quickly came to some decision about what I meant, because his face crumpled, and he put his hand on my shoulder. "I think Bishop Jonah was wrong about you, child," he murmured, and that sent a confusing flare of heat into my belly. Stuck somewhere between the want for praise and the urge to squirm out from under this man's touch, I stood paralysed and smiling.

Bishop Jonah knew what you were. Bishop Jonah could smell it; sulphuric desire wafting from your pores.

This man was no different, and I could not trust him.

He slipped his hand away. He answered my question finally with, "No. Not here. There are far worse things, certainly. But this abbey does not house them."

Which wasn't what I wanted to hear. I wanted the ease of access, I wanted it to be right under my fingertips; I wanted to be able to tear hell open at my doorstep so I might crawl easily into Asmodeus' cruel embrace.

But if it wasn't possible? If I had to travel, and search, and dedicate more years of my life to the cause? The fire of my desperation raged in my gut, and the fear and distress of waiting—of more years slipping away, of the last stretch of my youth dashed upon the rocks, its innards rotting, God, all I wanted was to be had and had roughly, all I wanted was for this body to be *worth something*, I wanted pleasure, I wanted to be fucked--!

Bishop Fazio touched me, and I jolted. Nausea threatened to erupt. I thought about vomiting over the edge of this wall.

"That upsets you," the bishop commented.

He had no idea. *Keep him on your side. Play the devout and pious follower of Christ; make deception and trickery your prayer.*

I let my voice shake. "Because. . ."

Enticed, he leaned forward, pulled by the quiver in my voice; the innocence and the piety he could lord over. "Because what?"

I dragged my body back over the warm stone and turned to look at the bishop. How I had moved meant I had to crane to look at him. The sun set his hair alight, haloing him, and I let myself feel holy and righteous in my deception. "Because the demon. . .I know they lie, bishop. I know there is trickery afoot. But it said someone was trying to open a gate into hell itself."

His jaw clenched so tightly that I could see the movement.

I averted my gaze, but his hand moved forward. Forefinger to chin, he tilted my gaze back to his.

"Don Alessandro," he murmured. "You have done us a great service. You have warned us of something terrible."

I swallowed. I saw what could happen next. He would leave. He would escalate things; he would whisper things up the chain of command until even the pope knew, and I would be stuck here, having made things worse for myself.

"We must take every illicit tome that is here, and move it somewhere safer," I said.

To my great relief, the bishop nodded. "There is a place."

He stared out at the ocean again, tone shifting, edging towards something apologetic. "I would. . .I would hate to disturb your life here, but—"

"I have been called," I said quickly. I shot to standing; I could not hide my eagerness. "Please," I said, without regret, without shame. "Let me do this."

And he looked at me and blessed me with, "Yes, you shall come," and my heart raced with the same ferocity as a charge of horses, and briefly, I found God again, just to say: *Thank you for your trusting servants. Thank you for all your fools.*

Asmodeus.

I am coming.

Two

We were a band of holy men and servants crammed into a gig and on horseback, galloping to a destination I did not know the name of. Bishop Fazio rode out with such haste that I barely had to bother with farewells; I told Oliviero not to worry, that I would make things right, and I silently hoped I would never see him again.

The only thing I took besides the clothes on my back was the letter opener I had used to cut the palm of my hand when I'd summoned Asmodeus. Partly out of sentiment, and partly out of necessity; if I was this far gone, then thinking that I *wouldn't* go so far to defend myself should I be discovered was idiotic.

I would go to any lengths to take Asmodeus' cock again.

"It will take two days to get there," Bishop Fazio told me. His body bumped and shuddered as the gig clattered over the uneven road out of my small town.

The sun set in a red bleed across the horizon, and the colour reminded me of what I did to summon Asmodeus to me. The sticky slickness of blood against my cock. The way it dried fast and uneven. My fingers glided over the healed cut on my palm with a tremor. A thunderous desire clapped through me.

"Pray," Bishop Fazio whispered, mistaking the look on my face. The gig had crates full of the abbey's more dangerous tomes, and they rattled and slid towards me with every bump of the ride. But I wasn't worried—I had no fear of them. It felt like being amongst brethren, in a strange way. As if I was amongst like-minded folk.

I had more camaraderie with these illicit papers than with my flesh and blood brethren.

To pass the time, I did close my eyes, and I did pray, in a way. To It, though, and not to Him. I thought of its body. I thought of its hot breath along my neck. I thought of the way it might bend me over and split me open when I finally walked into Hell.

When we arrived out our destination, I was surprised. Intrinsically I had expected we would be in the city; that Rome would be waiting with its ancient soul, that I would be before the Vatican and limited by its many measures. Instead, we were in another town.

Outside the gig window, the villagers stopped to watch us gallop past. They lowered their scythes and buckets, and then the village itself enveloped us with its warm, bright stone and patchwork tiles. But we sped through this town, too, spilling out the other side, and suddenly a lake greeted us. The gig stopped abruptly. The water was quiet and unmoving. The lake was tucked away behind another lake, set in a volcanic crater. Vineyards spilled out around the blue bastion and up the slope to where the gig had paused, these green fields sprawling over terraces down the natural incline. Reeds swayed gently in the breeze, and the sun felt warm and inviting. A peaceful place. Not the source of hellish information. Not what I needed at all.

I looked at Bishop Fazio. "Here?"

His brow collapsed at my incredulous tone, and he grunted, that familiar, unimpressed expression clouding his face. "Here," he repeated, knocking on the roof of the gig. He looked at me and said nothing more. I could feel the crates pressing in on either side, and under his gaze, the fear I had been long ago trained to feel blared to life like a warning bell, and each toll of it sent shivers into my gut. Immediate claustrophobia clawed at my throat, but I waited in tense silence for the child servant to open the door. A blustery cool breeze swirled into the gig and sent my hair flying every which way, but I breathed it in, let it settle in my lungs.

You are close. Do not grow scared now.

Pleasure. Pleasure so whole and intense I might feel as if I was beyond my body. I might reach a state beyond mortality; beyond humanity; beyond *me.*

It would be worth it. I wanted—I wanted it.

Despite the shame, despite the little voice in me that screamed and thrashed about, tempting me away from sin, tempting me back to goodness and primness, the cage of the church, the manacles of my rigid faith, I wanted to be used.

I wanted to be fucked.

"Let us go, then," I said, and left the gig.

———

By some holy miracle, we spoke to no one, and no one spoke to us. The townsfolk went to great strides to avoid us altogether, fleeing from our line of sight as if we were an incoming plague, and I wondered what it would mean to them to see men in the draperies and trappings of holy servants. I imagined anywhere else, how the people would have celebrated. How we might have been welcomed. But here, they seemed to see us and shrink away.

We became a procession weaving our way down that slope towards the still lake at the bottom. Marching single file, I trailed behind Bishop Fazio, who, despite walking slowly and clumsily, seemed to be enjoying the walk.

"What do you know of the myths, Don Alessandro?" he called back to me. The servants around us led us on, clearing a path, showing us where to walk to avoid becoming trapped in the tangling vineyard paths.

I ducked my head. "I do not engage with such pagan fantasies," I said—which was true. I didn't know much of anything, except where it related to Christianity; how God found the Romans, and the tensions that ensued.

"Do you know where we are?"

"No," I said truthfully.

"Naples. The bay of Naples."

A name even I knew, for the volcano Vesuvius, and for the towns it destroyed. "Why here?" I asked. Pleaded, really—I wanted no more of these games, no more of these questions. I wanted—Asmodeus.

But the bishop gave me no answer. We trudged down the rest of the slope in silence. At the bottom, the lake rippled out, peaceful and unmoving. Nothing appeared wrong with it. Ducks floated on the surface. A warm breeze moved through the air, and the whole scene seemed cast in a warm-green haze; it felt, in every way, like summer.

Bishop Fazio glanced at me. "Do not be fooled by its peace," he said. "I have brought you to Lake Avernus."

The name meant nothing to me, and I shook my head. The bishop nodded and craned his neck back at the sky. "The myths say it is an entrance to the underworld. That here, in a cave—they call it the 'Cave of the Sibyl'—lies a gate to Hell itself."

He spoke calmly, but with a disdainful edge to his voice, and he would not meet my gaze as he said it. He spoke looking up at the sky, like God might be watching, like he had to prove to the Holy Father he meant no harm speaking so freely of pagan myths and hell gates.

But my heart began to race. I had to stop myself from laughing. I thought: *could it be so easy?* But why on earth would the bishop be leading me here?

He caught the look on my face and tutted. "Fear not. The locals still avoid it—they do not approach the cave, and certainly do not enter it."

"Enter it?" I said, glancing at the lake, but he shook his head and stalked onwards. For another five odd minutes we walked, crushing through underbrush and overgrown grass, and hidden beneath the mess of foliage sat the yawning chasm of a cave mouth.

My heart jolted.

I looked to the bishop but received no further relief from him. His brow furrowed and he gave the order—not for just anyone to walk inside, but for he and I to go.

I glanced back at the servants, feeling exposed and naked without them. How silly. I craved this moment, and yet...

"Come," the bishop said.

I understood belatedly as we pushed inside. The light disappeared, swallowed by the infernal dark, and whether Bishop Fazio believed it or not, I felt something in my soul shiver. As if the mortal part of me could sense the change, a tingling pain began to throb in my forehead, and the longer we pushed forward into the dark cavern, the less I felt connected to myself. He struck something against the stone wall and a blaze of firelight sparked to life. Soft orange light pulsed over the walls. Water dripped from the walls and a dank smell permeated from the ground, and then abruptly I was walking over a sheet of waxed canvas—expensive and fairly new.

The bishop kept walking, but I stopped. He reached down and dragged another canvas tarp from its place, and as the light spilled over the central cavern I saw it all revealed: huge chests stacked upon another and bolted with heavy locks.

My heart thudded.

"We will put them here," Bishop Fazio said.

It wasn't enough just to dump those now useless tomes in this graveyard. I needed to find that particular tome, the one that could tear this world asunder and give me what I wanted.

"It's not. . ." I started.

The bishop turned. "What?"

"It's not enough, Bishop Fazio. You. . .I am sorry, but you must realise that."

He raised the torch to me. The motion meant shadows danced over his face, pooling deeply in the trenches beneath his eyes.

"You think this is not enough?"

"I know it. These should be. . . the tome to open the Gates of Hell shouldn't be here, in front of a Gate to Hell!"

"It is just a myth, Don Alessandro." His voice took on a dangerous edge. "Surely you do not believe this pagan nonsense? It is the best place to hide things. No locals come searching here."

I was surprised, in a way, by his surety. I wanted him to be swayed, to be frightened. I ended up saying, "Let us take it to Rome. To the Vatican. Let us be sure and make it safe."

He scanned my face and sighed, but eventually nodded. Relief flooded me. The bishop placed the torch in a sconce I hadn't noticed and dusted off his hands away from his holy robe.

"That one," he said, pointing to one of the chest. "Haul it

out for me, would you? You are still so young. My body cannot do it."

I tried to keep the eagerness from my step as I launched forward and hefted the chest out with all my might. My muscles strained and that good ache started up in my joints, and it reminded me of waking the day after Asmodeus was done with me, and feeling the pressure in my spine, the jolt in my neck, and throbbing ache in my hole.

The bishop moved his robe to the side and revealed a ring set of keys, which he unclipped and handed to me.

"Wrap it up in this," he murmured, pulling a cloth from somewhere unseen. "I had thought. . ." he shook his head. "You are right. I should have listened to my instincts earlier."

I didn't know what he meant, not really, but I took the cloth readily anyway and hesitated on my knees before the chest. Very carefully, I put the key in the slot. I breathed in, found a holy reverence in that tension, and put my intention into the unlocking of the chest.

This is a deliberate sundering. Here marks my complete betrayal for my brethren, for humanity, for this world. I want Asmodeus more than I want salvation. Let it be known.

The air shifted as I opened that chest, and its creak sounded like a waking groan as I inhaled the stuffy, long stagnant air that had lived inside it for years. I didn't need the bishop to tell me which one it was. Something happened in my vision, and I could see nothing else but that old, leatherbound tome, as if a vignette had fallen around me and tunnelled my focus towards it.

The tome itself was nothing special. The paper had a thick quality to it, closer to something woven together than what I was used to. The cover was a supple leather, grey and stained, and no title had been embossed onto the manuscript, and yet I knew.

The bishop's breath shuddered. "How did you. . ."

"It is my purpose," I said, clutching it in my hands. I tried and failed to keep to the shake from my voice.

He misheard me, misunderstood—like this was God warning me of evil, entrusting me to keep this tome safe. But the hot pull in my stomach, a warmth expanding behind my belly button, proved to me this was the work of something greater.

I put faith in that feeling and opened the manuscript. Even though the light was dull, I squinted hard to spy the words unfurling on the page. The script was stilted and small, written in a rushed hand—

Tuum desiderium probare debes, ut ianuam vorantem inferi aperias.
    Effunde cruorem, et sparsa in moenia tendit.
    Clama voce desiderii tui.
    Mortalem linque vitam.

Which meant:

You must prove your desire in order to open the yawning gate of hell.
    Pour out the blood, and let it be spread onto the walls.
    Call out with the voice of your desire.
    Give up your mortal life.

I looked up at the bishop. In the light cast by the flame, that flickering, undulating warmth, I must have looked deranged. A man on the verge of falling apart from his hunger. I felt ravenous. Desire scorched my insides; you understand, don't you? You understand why I had to do what I did. There was only one way to open the gates to hell, and the path had been laid out in front of me. So, too, had Bishop Fazio—who had led me here, like a sheep leading itself to the slaughter. I felt the weight of the letter opener at my side, and I stood so abruptly I spooked him.

"What. . .what are you doing?" he whispered.

I shook my head as I wrapped the tome in the cloth he had given me, held it gingerly, and passed it him. He took it from me, grip firm but shaking.

"It frightens me," I said, which wasn't wholly untrue. He still—trusted me. I know this because of the way his lip curled up and he gnawed at his lip, a deep noise blooming in his chest.

"As it should," he said, and he made to reach back for the torch. "Close the chest. We will retrieve and add your abbey's tomes to this collection, and then we will—"

He had his back turned, and this was the kindness I could allow him. The letter opener fit well in my hand. Its weight felt correct, a tool I was meant to have and hold and use. I brought it to the side of Bishop Fazio's neck and, like the spirit had moved me, sent its dull edge into his neck.

For a moment, I couldn't be sure what had happened. He dropped the torch, and all light was snuffed out. Only the shocked gurgles told me I had been successful. Weakly he clawed at the air around my head, attempting to reach back, to grip me, to stop me, but it was too late for him. He was dying, and I—I was on the edge of becoming something greater.

The emotion in me then felt flat, as if all the fear and worry I might have had about ending the bishop's life had been trapped behind some foggy layer in my heart. I had only the excitement, the urge to keep moving. Shucking the top layer of my robe, I lowered myself to the ground, where the bishop's blood had begun to pool and congeal with the dirt in a bloody mud. I coated my hands with it and stood, smearing it over the walls, returning to the still-twitching body to collect more and coating the other side. When it was done I went to my knees, facing the wall where the church's most illicit tomes had lived for years untouched, and I spoke out into the darkness:

"I want to open the gates of hell!"

Nothing. Nothing happened. I flushed, overwhelmed by the stupidity, by the insanity of what I was doing. The mortal in me floundered. I had committed a cardinal sin. I had killed, killed with glee, more willingly than I had done most anything in my life.

Nothing was happening. I had nothing to show for my actions. Bishop Fazio's blood was mixing with the dirt; I couldn't look at him, lest I lost my nerve. Fear pricked at my skin. The fear of being caught, of being punished *here* by the church, and not by some demonic presence. Not my body pushed to its limits, stretched and wanting.

I pushed my hair back, staining my forehead with blood in my attempt to wipe away sweat, and shouted: "Open!"

Nothing.

My stomach twisted. *Stupid. You are a stupid man.*

Bile crawled up my throat as I thrashed about in the dirt. Dust rose in clouds around me.

"Open the gates to hell!" I screamed. "Open them now!"

My voice returned to me in echoes, rebounding off the cave walls. Each time my voice came back tinny and thin, weaker with its desire, until it faded away, eaten by the cave. I was left with the stark reality of how pathetic I had become, and I spread my hands in the dirt, trying and failing to maintain my sanity.

Control your breathing. Trust in that demon: trust in how it wants to make you squirm. This waiting was a torment in its own right, an ultimate drawing out of my desire, and I believed Asmodeus would revel in seeing me like that, on my knees, so desperate for it that I had killed a man, a vessel of faith, a final nail in the coffin of my priesthood.

But I had forsaken God wholly. Why was the demon not hearing me? Why was I being forsaken in return?

"Please! *Asmodeus, please!*"

Desperate, embarrassing—my voice cracked. Down the cave vestibule I heard the answering question, shrill and faint. "*Bishop Fazio? Is everything alright?*"

I whipped my head back to the blood-smeared wall and tried again. "Open. *Open.* I want it. I will give everything up! *Please!*"

And still nothing happened. Was that—were those footfalls? I strained to hear the crunch of dirt underfoot, and upon hearing it began to panic.

They were coming. The servants of the bishop and the church and of God would find me and the bishop's corpse like this, and that would be the end. I would never have a chance again. I would never see Asmodeus—I would never be touched like that again.

No, no.

It hit me quickly.

The tome had told me what to do in no uncertain terms.

Give up your mortal life.

Fear burned hotly in me, but desire burned hotter. I crawled over to the bishop's body and wrenched the letter opener from his neck. A spray of arterial blood coated my hand in warmth, and a primal terror sparked in me. By this point though I had been so scared for so long that I ascended beyond the grip of my terror and landed somewhere close to apathy. Or rather, a singular focus drove me, and all distracting emotion seeped away until I was a vessel for my purpose.

I pulled back towards the centre of the cavern, unsure what to do with myself. Unsure now that I knew what I truly had to do. But without fear, it became easier to think.

I imagined opening my guts. I remembered the feeling of Asmodeus inside me and the way those claws pressed against the skin of my stomach. How easily it could have punctured me, then. How easy it would have been to spill my internal organs, to have them cascade out in a steaming, looping mess across the ground. Asmodeus would have used that new hole, I had no doubt; it did not care for me, not in the slightest. And this lack of care—this true apathy, which sat in such stark contrast to God's divine and endless love—aroused me more than anything else.

It wouldn't care that I had killed myself to get back to its embrace. I would call be pathetic. It would humiliate me; it would laugh at my true and inescapable desperation. But I would do it anyway. I had to.

I raised the letter opener to my heart, pulled back, and—

A rumbling sounded just as I pierced the side of my chest.

Panicked, I drew the blade back quickly and dropped it. I stood in a rush. Blood trickled down my chest, not enough to worry about but enough that the wound stung, the area around it throbbing.

The cave shook heavily. Dust and rocks dislodged and cascaded, and the ground shook. I was flung to the side, cheek scraping against the wall. Behind me, shouts and screams reverberated through the tunnel, and in an act of unholy providence, the mouth of this chamber disappeared in a matter of seconds. Rocks and rubble collapsed and closed it up perfectly, entombing me in my decision. I turned back to the cave wall, which had ruptured. Cracks sundered the rock wall apart. From between the fissures, the smell of sulphur wafted out; my mind jolted towards it, encouraged by the reminder of Asmodeus, the smell of it, and how entwined with my own arousal the scent had become.

Heat, a pulsing light, and a deep thrumming sound grew in the now suffocating chamber. I pushed off the wall as the shaking stabilised, and though dust and small rocks still rained down, I got close enough to feel the scorch of heat against my cheeks. The smell of sulphur was strong, and the fumes were suddenly overpowering. Every inhale singed my throat, and even my lungs began to feel impossibly tight. When my vision blurred and a great weightlessness spun through my head, I realised I was dying.

But there was nothing to be done. A second later, my vision went. The depths of unconsciousness claimed me.

Three

I woke with my soul on fire.

There is no other way to describe that feeling, except a complete internal scalding. I jolted up with a scream and went to tear off my cassock—except I already had, and was now in only breeches, smeared with my own blood and that of Bishop Fazio.

I sat on my knees and blinked away the pain, which came in ebbs and flows and never quite went away. The heat burned intensely in my stomach, pulled taut behind my belly button, almost like a cramp—but the pain was not wholly unwelcome.

Around me, the world burned. Smoky fog shielded most things from my view, and the ground was little more than the cave dirt I'd previously been lying in. But everything was cast in an orange haze, and everything smelled of burning. A cacophony of cries sounded, though distance made them made soft and faint like an ambient rustling. I inhaled deeply and felt my ribs expand, lungs inflating with air and sulphur and brimstone and smoke.

For all intents and purposes, I felt alive. I *was* alive—the wound still stung at my neck. I could feel pain, I needed to breathe. The only indication that anything at all had happened was the scenery, and the more I looked, the more I could see very little but the red haze, the more thrill I felt.

Inside me, a war started up between the anxiety and the excitement. I had so thoroughly forsaken my old life that I was now stranded in this place. With no guide, and no direction, I stood unmoored. Ridiculous and lost.

I thought: *You felt a pull to Asmodeus. You knew what you had to do. Surely you can feel that again.*

But when I closed my eyes and tried to feel that guiding feeling to the demon, nothing happened. I wondered if it ever had—if that calling I had been so sure was urging me here had simply been my own desire, so hot and fierce it allowed me to overcome my fear and shame.

My stomach throbbed. I groaned and bent over it, and since there seemed nothing else to be done, I started to walk, trying my best to ignore the overwhelming sense of guilt, regret, and embarrassment. For a seemingly endless stretch of time, I did nothing but wander through that red haze. No landmarks emerged. The sounds did not shift around me, so no matter how long I walked, the distant cries of screaming sounded neither closer nor further.

An ambient limbo, a liminal moment, a walking purgatory—the new fear in me burned as hotly as the pain in my stomach, as hot as the latent arousal I felt building inside my core. I worried inherently that this would be my punishment for all I had done to get here, and that I had been tricked so thoroughly that I had willingly condemned myself to and endless walk towards nothing. Sweat pooled at the back of head and wetted my hair. Would this be it?

I don't know how long I walked. I managed to push the fear and the upset away, convincing myself that moving forward was better than giving up and standing still. No thoughts went through my mind, no prayers or hopes. I kept myself an empty vessel.

Until I heard the voice.

"What on earth have you done now?"

Deep, familiar, frightening. Not Asmodeus. Yet it still resonated with me, booming through my body, and an old fear was pricked to life by it. The voice belonged to someone who had been in my early life, whom I hadn't seen in years. I stopped in my tracks and spun. The mists parted as a figure moved through them, a shrouded shape resolving into a man.

It was Bishop Jonah.

It wasn't the first time I'd heard his voice in so many years. Asmodeus had spoken with his inflection, too; had worn that man's vocal chords like a costume to pluck at my sensitivities, so that I would become pliable to the demon's wishes. Obedient. When I had been younger, Bishop Jonah had trained me like a dog to expect scolding and punishments—and he had apparently trained me so well that now my body fell into old habits. Anxiety sparked in me, and I turned rigidly to face the man.

But with the trick having already been played on me once, I hesitated.

"Nothing to say?" he stepped through the fog fully. He looked at once how I remembered him over the years, oscillating from the man of thirty-something who had taken me into his flock, knowing I was a thief, and over time growing to suspect I was a sodomist in the making, to the man in his early fifties, the age he'd been when he died.

He stood taller than me, his tanned skin thick like leather and well-lined. White hair sat cropped close to his skull, and his face stretched in a permanent scowl, resembling Bishop Fazio's eternal disgust. Without the softness leant by fat to Bishop Fazio's face and body, Bishop Jonah's expression tilted closer to pure hatred than disappointment. Years of anger and callousness had sculpted this permanent expression. I hadn't recalled it to be quite so severe and wondered if Hell had managed to age him; if he was, every so slowly, getting older and more decrepit. The oscillating image of him settled to the ageing man, still spritely enough to stand and walk, though this version of him leaned upon a cane, which he had just begun to use in life. Now his gnarled hand gripped his support and his knuckles popped, veins framing them, arthritic fingers shaking from the force. I thought: *What a true and persistent Hell*. Old age drawn out across eternity.

In his gaze sat a fury enhanced by the flames of Hell, which danced in the gossamer-thin whites of his eyes. I fought not to flinch away—for in that expression was years upon years of discipline—and I failed. My body feared him. I stepped back in the dirt.

Bishop Jonah's face twitched unkindly. Was he a demon in disguise? I flinched away from him once more. What game was being played?

But even as my mind worked to unstitch the fetid fear unspooling in my body—*you are beyond this man, now. He has no control over you! You belong to Asmodeus, Prince of Lust!*—I found myself responding like a child. My jaw clenched and my stomach twisted. Beneath his holy gaze, I felt sinful. An infernal, abominable mess.

He will see what you've done to get here, just as he saw what you are from the start.

I never knew exactly what it was he saw in me that other holy men didn't. I never knew how he had been so sure. Had God whispered the truth in his ears? Was Bishop Jonah so pure, so close to God, that he could spy the corruption knitted into my soul, or the way my skin would writhe with desire when the right man glanced at me?

"Filthy Alessandro," he spat over his shoulder now. His saliva met the earth and the dust darkened immediately around the wetness. "It surprises me not at all to find you here."

Bishop Jonah. It was... truly him?

I swallowed heavily. "You're in Hell."

"Astute as always," he growled, real vitriol coating his words like venom. He flashed me a look, a once over with a gaze that lingered a little too long on my naked chest. He glanced away to say, "Tell me. I was right, wasn't I? That you are. . ."

He didn't finish the question. He didn't have to.

I recalled the seconds after I finished my confessions, special times where Bishop Jonah himself had been the one to hear all the priesthood's sins. These were times where I never exposed all my thoughts, where I knew I had to keep things to myself. Memories of the tense silence returned to me now, the waiting seconds that stretched after my concluding *Amen.* The way the booth creaked as Bishop Jonah shifted inside.

"Is that all, Alessandro?"

Again, now, years and entire states of being removed, my body panicked with remembered shame. I breathed through it, biting my tongue. I heard Asmodeus instead, like the bells of a church drowning out the dead bishop's venom. I heard the voice as it had called to me that day with holy vigour, asking me, *"What had God's love given you except shame? What had God ever done for you?"*

"Am I a sodomist?" I murmured. "Only very recently."

Which was true. I was Asmodeus' bitch—and, so far, its alone.

The bishop narrowed his eyes. "You smell different to everything else here. Sweet, like life. Everything here smells and tastes. . .wrong. Like the flavour is on the tip of my tongue, but not quite there. A distant memory."

He stared at me, expecting an answer. I gave him nothing.

Bishop Jonah's face imploded. "You are not dead, are you, Alessandro?"

I decided to walk past him. This man was only a distraction to me, whether he was real or not. It was Asmodeus I wanted. Asmodeus I craved. I walked—

--and fell crashing to my knees as the bishop's cane knocked my legs out from under me.

The ground rushed up to meet my face. Dust burst into my open mouth and made me choke.

I rolled as I heard him approach. The bishop's cruel smile shone down on me like the sun. "Little priest. Lamb to the slaughter. You opened the gates so willingly."

I coughed and tried to sit up, but Bishop Jonah used the end of his cane to shove me back into the dust. Heat pulsed in my spine where the warm earth met my skin, and the force of the bishop's cane made my breathing shallow.

"You opened the gates."

"Yes," I spat. My voice came out weak and wheezing, but I summoned the anger I held deep in my chest; years of repression! Years of self-hating and shame and anger! How much of that could be attributed to this man? How much of it had festered because of the way he looked at me?

"I am here for Asmodeus. I am here to embrace what you have condemned me for. Let me go: you are not a holy man any longer. Hell has claimed you too!"

Surprisingly, his cane moved aside. I rolled out and pushed up to stand, but the Bishop called out:

"You didn't think it would be that easy, did you? That Asmodeus, Prince of Lust, a King of Hell, would be waiting for you so eagerly? You are just another sack of meat for it to pleasure itself with—surely you can understand that?"

I understood it and felt at once a confusing mix of arousal and hurt. That I was nothing more than something for the demon's pleasure stirred that low heat in me. But I was human, and even with logic and reasoning and an intrinsic understanding that I meant nothing to the demon, my gut roiled in protest.

I wanted Asmodeus to want me the same.

"Stop running from me, Alessandro," the bishop said. And his tone dropped somewhere strange and inviting.

I turned around. "What?"

"You want to find the path to Asmodeus. Without my help, you will be cursed to wander this land forever. You will get nowhere. You will never find him. You will never have that pink hole of yours stretched to gaping again."

My heart thudded. Heat rushed to me cheeks; I couldn't meet his eye without seeing a decade of history play out before me. I hated that he could see me and know what I wanted. I hated that he could say those words and my body would react with both fear and a jolting twitch in my cock. I hated—I hated that it was *Bishop Jonah* saying this to me.

I asked, "Are you really him? Or are you some demon?"

He did not answer right away. Seconds passed as the soft clop of the cane sounded in the dirt. I trembled. The bishop's fingers brushed over my cheek. Wrinkled and coarse, he pulled me to face him. His breath curled warm over my face; confusion bloomed in me. How—how could *that*—affect me?

"Oh, Alessandro," Bishop Jonah purred. "Does it matter?"

My throat closed up and went thick with my fear. What could I say to that? Whether this Bishop Jonah was truly him or not, I had the fear and the cautious respect for him that I'd fostered my entire young adult life. My organs reacted to him the same. My breathing felt erratic. Sweat pricked at my skin. And somehow, caught in the limbo of my fear and my desire, I felt a shudder that dipped low and deep inside me.

Bishop Jonah's hand moved fast from my cheek to my

chin. He gripped me hard, hard enough I could feel the bones being crushed and the meat of my lower cheeks aching.

"Do what I say, and I will tell you how to find the Prince of Lust."

Tell me why a fierce loyalty illuminated my insides then. I shoved back, slapping the bishop's hand away. "No," I said. "I made a promise. I am—I am Asmodeus' pet."

"You are warm flesh to fuck into. It would fuck your corpse if it wanted to; you, as a person, cannot mean a thing to it."

And I remembered Asmodeus telling me, *"Plenty of demons in Hell, my pathetic little priest."*

Suddenly I felt like I possessed a sacred duty.

Perhaps lust overrode my defiance, or perhaps I believed entirely in this new religious purpose. And it *was* religious; Asmodeus and the experiences I had with it felt religious to me. I had this understanding that bloomed in my chest that however this played it, it was a test—and I was expected to play a part.

Bishop Jonah—or the demon wearing his face, I still couldn't be sure—saw the shift in my gaze. His face lifted fractionally, and then a smile burst through that ugly, furious expression. He laughed and laughed and let go of my chin, which ached from the pressure of his grip. Then, before he said anything, before I had a chance to follow any of his instructions, he whacked the cane over both my thighs and sent me dropping onto my knees.

Pain shuddered through my kneecaps and up my thigh, and at the look on my face—defiant, rageful—the bishop struck me across the face with that wooden cane again.

I yelped. My vision blurred with tears and a whited-out shock. The pain felt blistering. My teeth throbbed and went biting down into my tongue. The cheek itself screamed with pain. The bishop leaned down and grabbed my face again.

Unkindly, he spat. I closed my eyes but felt the spray of saliva dribbling over the curve of my face. My body shivered, confused with its arousal.

He smiled at me. That smile, I will tell you, shocked me. I realised I had never seen such a look of joy contort the bishop's face. That it was aimed at me—that it was aimed at me when I was like *this*?

The bishop nodded his head. "You already know your place," he said. He brought his foot forward and ground his shoe over my cock.

I groaned and rocked forward, splaying both hands on the ground. Already painfully hard—and shameful about it, so shameful, so bitingly concerned I felt nauseous—the bishop's touch sent both pleasure and pain sparking through my body.

"St-stop this," I grunted, but even to myself, my voice sounded airy and faint. Distant with pleasure.

The bishop tutted. Using his cane, he shifted my chin up to look at him.

"Alessandro, you have always wanted to be treated like this. I knew it when I was alive, and I know it now. The only difference here is that you have proven it so willingly. You have killed to get here. Your body smells of blood, and life, and desire—you *want* this. Whether I am a lesser demon, or whether I am your Bishop Jonah, doesn't really matter to you. In the end, what your body sees, what your body reacts to, is a desire for the depraved." He stepped forward. I swallowed intrinsically. My heart raced. Conflicted, sitting somewhere between pleasure and fear, want and distress, I struggled to keep his gaze. "You may have never wandered about sucking my cock before now, but you are pathetic, and wanting, and if I tell you to open your mouth, I know you will do it."

I didn't do it. Not right away. I focused on slowing my breathing, which was rapid fire and inconsistent. I struggled to think—was he right? Had I ever wanted the bishop? Or had I wanted his respect? His trust? His love? Were those such clear distinctions to me?

If I could have none of that, but I could still be of use to him, would I do it? Would I allow my throat to be fucked here, on my knees in this hellish limbo?

Would I do it for myself? Or for Asmodeus?

This part of me still clung to reasoning and logic. I still wanted to be a human man, bound up in morality, bargaining with oneself to avoid the guilt and shame so familiar to me. But now, after what I had done to Bishop Fazio, and the complete rejection of a life dedicated to God, why did I still feel this way?

I hadn't replied to the bishop. He tutted and cocked his head and said, "Take the rest of your clothes off, Alessandro."

I quivered. I felt my cock straining. Without touch, it felt warm and firm and twitching. The skin of the glands felt dotted with pleasure, vibrating with it. I wanted to touch myself. I wanted—something more.

I looked up at Bishop Jonah, who was not a pretty man by any stretch of the imagination, but he was familiar. A man who had commanded my respect and my fear for years now had me on my knees. . .

I could pretend I was doing this for the demon Asmodeus. If I wanted to be split open on its cock again, I would have to find it, somewhere in amongst this place. But Hell was large, ever expanding, and full of its demonic brethren—it was an unknowable place for mortals. If I couldn't exchange my body for the help of demons, then what could I offer them? Why else would beasts of evil choose to aid in my cause?

Perhaps I. . .had to do this.

The bishop laughed. I jolted in place, pulled back from my anxious reasoning to this reality, where my knees ached, and dust covered me. Bishop Jonah bared his teeth. I felt like I had at thirteen, fourteen. Terrified of him. Terrified of the feelings that kept growing in my gut. The bishop leaned forward and tapped my chin again. The touch—warm, calloused, unkind—made me gasp.

"Oh, I know that look. You are trying to convince yourself that, if you truly think about it, there is a moral need for you to open your mouth and let me slide inside."

I blinked at him. If my face could get any hotter, I'm sure it happened then.

"After everything," the bishop continued, "I have to wonder. Do you still need to convince yourself to do things, Alessandro? Or will you just *do* what you wish and bear the consequences?"

My heart thudded in my chest. The nausea in me gave way to a giddy release, because I knew, in my heart of hearts, that he was right. What consequence would there be for this action except Hell, a place I had already welcomed? I had killed a holy man and forsaken God so thoroughly and publicly that there could be no redemption.

Stop fighting it, my gut said, my heart pleaded, my mind cooed. It didn't matter who touched me. It didn't matter what they looked like. I wanted to be had and used and wanted; I wanted this vessel to be made useful.

Bishop Jonah saw me relax and stopped laughing, though that all-knowing smile could not be so easily dislodged. With a fervour, he shifted his cassock aside, and pulled himself free.

The layers of the priestly cloth had obscured it, but he was excited, as hard I was. My mind went blank momentarily. I forgot who he was, his age, his appearance—I forgot everything except that I was on my knees and that someone had their cock out for me to suck. Another part of my mind, long tethered and controlled, slipped forward the way it had with Asmodeus. I found it easy to let go and did nothing to stop him as he walked forward.

He smelled of sweat. He gripped his cock, flushed pink at the tip, averagely long but with ample girth, and he pressed it against my face. I closed my eyes with my heart racing, inhaling the smell of the underside of his cock, and sucked a ball into my mouth. It had flavour—sweat and unwash, not unwholly unpleasant—and in fact, the added degradation of having the bishop drag his unclean self over my face only made me shiver more.

"Pathetic," the bishop said, and I groaned as I sucked. He hissed and wrapped his fingers into my hair, pulling hard, and then he wrenched me off. His ball left my mouth with a pop, and I only had time to say, "Ah!" before he shoved my mouth over his twitching cock.

The moan that left me was guttural, smothered by the blockage slowly pushing down my throat. Without care or ease, the bishop thrust hungrily into my mouth. I lasted five thrusts before I gagged, before the rapid motion in and out of my throat made my body convulse around the girth. The bishop groaned, rocking forward as the sides of my wet pharynx closed around him.

He pulled out calling the Lord's name. "God, oh Holy God," he said. I looked up at him and he slapped me hard across the face.

"You love this," he said, stepping his foot once more against my straining cock. "You disgrace the church with how much you love this. Tell me, Alessandro. Confess."

I didn't, not right away. I was still catching my breath. He used the moment of open-mouthed panting to press himself once more inside. Then he gripped a fistful of my hair and thrust. I tried to stay calm, to breathe around the blockage, to not gag, but he was so deep, and my throat was so full that tears gathered at the edges of my eyes. He stuffed himself into me, cock ramming down as deep as it would go, and a flood of saliva and bile pooled in my mouth. When the bishop dragged himself free, the wet mix dripped from my mouth and splattered into the dirt.

I moaned. I smelled of sex and want and sweat. My cock ached with desire; I could see it twitching through the breeches. Bishop Jonah's eyes glided down my chest and stomach hungrily, and he made a soft noise when his eyes saw my cock, but somehow his expression remained slightly close to disgust. Like all of this was a chore, like he enjoyed none of it. Like it was his duty to do this to me. To put me in my place.

"Take them off," he said.

I hesitated. He did not. The bishop's cane whacked across my chest, sending the skin aflame. My nipples throbbed but pushed up hard and obvious with want, and the bishop struck me again so hard I screamed. The sound of my voice echoed back, returned by the wall of fog that boxed us in, and the bishop shoved his cane beneath my chin, pressing the end into my jugular so firmly it became difficult to breathe.

"Do what I tell you, you pathetic excuse for a man."

Which made me move. I pushed up onto my knees and unlaced the black breeches, slipping them over my hips quickly and gracelessly. When I went to stand to push them over my ankles, the bishop laughed and struck me—across the ass.

I cried out and fell face first into the dirt, cock out and pressing against the warm dust, and pants tangled around my legs. The skin stung, but my whimper only seemed to embolden him, and he struck me again and again until I was writhing, pushing away uselessly towards nothing, and non-committal as I went. It hurt—it hurt, but I didn't want it to end. My mind spun somewhere happy and half-blank, and every strike against my flesh sent my soul stirring. It felt like he was beating against the shackles of my shame, like every strike weakened a link and pushed me ever closer to unabashed freedom.

As I lay there, precum weeping out of me and skin stinging, the bishop came and wrenched me up by my head.

"We aren't done, whore," he grunted. His cock twitched in my line of sight, and I pushed myself up greedily, mouth searching; pathetic, I knew I was, I knew how I must have looked with the dust around me stained and wet and congealing with my saliva. I felt desperate.

Then—perhaps I *wanted* to do this.

He pushed into my throat again and I groaned, licked, sucked. I went to touch myself, to rut against the palm of my hand, but he brough his booted foot down and crushed against my aching cock. Shamefully, I bucked up against the pressure, excited and eager for any kind of release. The edges of his black cassock ghosted across the skin of my forearms, and incense had long ago settled into the fabric, which was now forever scented by the old, stale sandalwood and frankincense. It sent me back to church and holy ceremonies, so that somehow now I felt close to divinity when I had never been further away. My eyes rolled to the back of my head as he thrust inside, his foot crushing down harder on my groin.

Abruptly, he pulled away. Stringy saliva and precum connected us. His cock rested on my face, the warm tip kissing my cheek, and with it the bishop lightly slapped my face, tried to call me back to the moment, and said, "Confess to me, little priest."

I swallowed hard, still trying to regulate my breathing, and looked up at him. On my knees like that, dog-like and eager, I felt so wonderfully apart of myself. There was none of that side of praying, where your soul began to feel distant, or where you yearned to be outside of your body and far beyond it, floating up above with God. I felt, right now, so particularly human that it made me joyous. I yearned not for heaven, but for this moment dragged out and extended and relived, where my body could offer pleasure, and where it could be degraded; where I could be depraved and love it.

I opened my mouth and whispered, "I have sinned."

"You have," came the reply, and three taps to my cheek had my mouth open and searching for him again. I chased after his cock with my lips, but he pulled away. "Stupid little slut that you are. You have betrayed God, haven't you?"

"Yes," I whispered. "Yes, I have. Willingly. Happily."

"Tell me."

"I opened the gate to Hell. I murdered a man. I did it. . .for Asmodeus."

The bishop tilted at his hips and slapped me hard across the face. He caught my ear, made it ring, and dull pain echoed through my skull. "You did it for cock."

"For cock," I repeated, nodding my head. My voice came out tinny and strangled. I breathed through the pain and nodded. Tears streaked my face. "For cock. I did it because I want cock."

"That's it," the bishop said. He had a fistful of my hair and, tugging it firmly, he made me nod. Up and down, as pliable as a doll, I nodded to him over and over. "You love this," he said, still making me nod. But the physical affirmation wasn't enough. "Say it!"

"I love it!" I gasped. "I love it! I love being used like this!"

"Used like what?"

"Like an animal!" I cried out. My cock throbbed as I said it. My cheeks were aflame, shame and pleasure mixing. "Like I was made only for this. To pleasure others."

He let go of me and stepped back, expression appraising, edging away from mindless disgust to something thoughtful. He cocked his head. I saw the visage slip momentarily, and he was Bishop Jonah ten years younger, the expression identical to how I remembered.

The memory that came to me then was odd, perverse in its

own way, and haunting in another. I was twenty-five, and I hadn't seen Bishop Jonah in years. I had not yet returned to the abbey of my village, and was worshipping elsewhere, a few towns over. The bishop came and saw me; saw right through me like he didn't remember me. He hadn't greeted me. He hadn't said a thing. My stomach had fallen far as his eyes passed over me. I recall thinking: *what?*

I couldn't reconcile it then, but I felt abandoned. I wanted him to remember me and know me; I wanted him to scold me for the creases in my cassock, I wanted to be seen. It didn't matter if he hated me.

I sought him out that night after mass, under the pretence of thanking him, when in reality I wanted to be remembered. I didn't find him that night. I didn't find him until he took confession for us, a great honour, and I had to confess that I felt jealous of the attention he was awarding other priests. That I felt upset he wasn't focusing on me.

"We are servants of God, before we are His children," the bishop had told me. And then, with a pained sigh, "Alessandro, you are one of many young men I have mentored in my time. Surely you knew that before now?"

I remember breathing heavily, not understanding the twist in my gut. He disliked me, and he had made my life a living hell, and here I was all desperate and wanting. Why? Why did I care? Why did I care so much that I felt hot in my cheeks, and fire in my gut? Looking back, I wonder if it was the knowledge he had of me, that deep down he knew what I was in truth, and perhaps with the right words or the right prayers, I thought he might be able to make me pure.

I was not attracted to him. Not physically. But the authority. . .the power he wielded. God's man on earth.

He might as well have been God to *me*.

Then, in Hell, blinking up at him through my eyelashes, with saliva dripping from my mouth, I shivered with expectation and understanding. His authority had followed me even here, and I was a slave to it once more. His eyes slid over me as I quivered before him on my knees. A smile pricked his sour expression apart.

"Touch yourself," he ordered. His tone took on that commanding cadence, reminding me of his sermons, which always sat halfway between moralising and worshipping, an attempt to impart both the wisdom of the holy text's teachings and God's love. I felt compelled to move and rocked back onto my haunches. Exposed like that, with my ankles straining against the breaches gathered at my ankles, my whole body shivered.

But I was too slow for the bishop. His face twisted and he slapped forward with his cane, slicing its blunt edge across my chest diagonally. Fire seared down my body and I cried out. Pain had me whimpering, and still my cock wept with precum. The bishop's cane lowered, the wooden bottom grazing over my skin until it dropped low enough that he could lightly slap the underside of my cock. It jumped with each touch of the cane, and I balled my hands into the dust by my shins, trying in vain to find purchase in the loose and shifting particles; trying to ground myself so I wasn't aroused so terribly by my own bishop.

You know as well as I do that I was never going to succeed.

I grunted. Suddenly, the light and the heat burned overwhelmingly, and I had to squeeze my eyes shut. Vulnerability crept over my skin like a shiver.

"Ah, ah," the bishop said. "Open your eyes."

I hesitated. Everything felt hot and upsetting and—too much for me. The feeling wasn't quite regret, but latent embarrassment still clung to me, heavy and tar-like, impossible to shake away. What I wanted butting up against my old-ingrained fear. . .it felt somehow easier to embrace Asmodeus, inhuman in its appearance and so utterly opposite of the church's values, than to do this before Bishop Jonah—or something that looked like him. This felt like a complete admission, a confession before the church, and something that would follow me. I could not excuse pleasuring myself before a man who had chastised me my whole life.

Bishop Jonah's voice cooed, "Give in to this, Alessandro. You are already here, in Hell. You have already given up your immortal soul. You cannot pretend to fear God's wrath now, and shame will hardly save you from the lustful creatures in this realm. So. . ."

He paused, long enough for the tension to spark in my stomach. Expectation tugged me forward.

"Why don't you just give in?"

I exhaled heavily. Erratic breathing. A heart rate so loud and fast I could hear it echo inside my ribcage. I fought to open my eyes, and in that time, the bishop moved so close I could feel his warm breath curl over my neck.

He whispered, "Open your eyes, Alessandro. Look at your bishop and do what you are told."

The throbbing at my crotch became so much to bear that I thrust up towards nothing, hoping to make friction with only the air. The bishop chuckled and that voice lulled me. I opened my eyes.

Blinking away my bleariness, I was greeted with the sight of the bishop pleasuring himself, hand moving up and down over the cock that peeked through his cassock. The blushed tip blinked at me between forefinger and thumb and the movement was hypnotic. My groin pulsed and with my gaze locked on his movements, on that cock of his straining and weeping and the little shivers of pleasure that kept jolting through his body, I moved my own hand and squeezed the base of my cock.

"Oh, fuck," I muttered.

I squeezed. The blood that had gathered there, and the

long stretch of time without touch, meant this simple action sent stars spinning behind my eyes. The bishop walked forward and spat—not on my face, but onto my cock, wetting it with his saliva. Each touch pushed the shame and fear further out of my mind, and I could thrust up into the palm of my hand, gliding against the skin as precum and saliva commingled.

"Ah, that's it," the bishop murmured. He stepped back and took in the sight of me fully. Meeting his eyes was difficult. I kept shuddering, closing my eyes for seconds at a time to regain some semblance of control, but at some point when the shock of the exposure and the vulnerability ebbed away, I could look more wholly. At that point, the expression on his face compelled me to stare. I watched the way he watched me; the way the speeds of his hand increased to match mine, the way his eyes clouded with distant pleasure, lust pushing him to look everywhere, to watch me fuck into my own hand with interest. And suddenly, we were staring at each other's eyes.

My cheeks burned. The feeling in my chest was an amalgamation, rolling between pleasure and fear; this vicious feeling that called forth all the shades of my youth. Every time he had yelled at me. Every time he had called me impure.

You stupid boy. . .a thief at heart. And here you are, thieving my time. My good will! The church's!

Or the voice of him, in confession, asking, *Alessandro, is that all you have to tell me?*

No. It wasn't. We both knew it back then and we both knew it in that moment.

I grunted and twitched, leaning back on one hand to thrust up with a renewed desperation. "I am a slut," I whispered.

"Louder," came the resounding command.

"I am a slut!"

My voice echoed back to me.

"A sodomist. I want it. . .crave it. . ."

"Crave *what?*"

"To be used."

My hand moved faster. Heat pooled and the pressure built, a coalescing of my body and its desires and its pleasure, until each touch felt clarifying: every stroke pushed me closer to the edge.

"Filthy," he said. "A disgrace."

"Yes."

"Then repent, Alessandro. Ask to be saved."

I jolted. I looked up at him in shock. What he asked of me felt like a greater sin than what I was doing now. He wanted me to speak to him like we were in confession. To ask God to forgive a sin I was in the middle of committing.

I glanced away—he moved quickly, knocking his cane against my face to drag me back to him.

"Do you need help remembering how to begin?"

I hesitated, swallowed, and shook my head. Against my cock, my movement slowed. Shame and fear threatened my erection—or so I expected. In truth, I only seemed to get harder. The humiliation made me dizzy.

I cleared my throat. "Contrition," I said, and nothing else. I didn't have to; the word carried a weight to it. To confess truly and be absolved, I had to be overcome by remorse for my sins. I looked up at the bishop. I recalled how I felt before Asmodeus. Very slowly, I shook my head. "I don't. . ."

I don't regret a thing.

"Ah, but you must," the bishop said. "Or I cannot absolve you of this sin, Alessandro."

I swallowed. I added the lie to the ever-growing list of my sins. I was lying to myself, to this bishop, to God by omission. Emboldened, further aroused somehow by the deception, my cock twitched in my hand. I squeezed it again, grunting.

"Bless me, Father, for I have sinned," I said. I tried to close my eyes, but the bishop's cane tapped beneath my chin. Flushing, I opened and stared up at him. "It has been months since my last confession. I accuse myself of the following sins. I have had lustful thoughts too many times to count."

"Mm."

My breath shuddered as a whisper of pleasure shot through me. "I have. . .summoned the demon Asmodeus. Twice. I have let it sodomise me. I have welcomed it. I enjoyed it. I have murdered your holy servant Bishop Fazio. I have let the promise of mortal pleasure lead me. I have let Bishop Jonah do this to me—"

"Fucking tart!" The bishop spat at my face and I flinched away. "You're the one who has tempted me."

Christ. Fuck. It shouldn't—I should not have been so affected, and yet, there I was, grinding up into my hand with increasing fervour, near delirious with how fast my heart was racing and the sweat that was beading at my forehead and dripping down into my eyes. "Yes, yes, I'm sorry. I have tempted Bishop Jonah and led him to sin!"

"Good boy," the bishop barked out a laugh and touched himself in earnest, eyes never straying from me.

With my pride dissolved, I arched my back and let the bishop see all of me in my naked glory.

"For these I ask pardon of God. I ask for penance and absolution."

"I will give you penance," the bishop said. "Act of Contrition. Say it now."

In stilted Latin, each word punctured by my rapid breath, I said it:

Deus meus, ex toto corde pænitet me omnium meorum peccatorum,

 eaque detestor, quia peccando,
 non solum pœnas a te iuste statutas promeritus sum,

sed præsertim quia offendi te,
summum bonum, ac dignum qui super omnia diligaris.
Ideo firmiter propono,
adiuvante gratia tua,
de cetero me non peccaturum peccandique occasiones proximas fugiturum.
Amen.

O My God, I am heartily sorry for having offended Thee,
and I detest all my sins, because I dread the loss of heaven and the pains of hell,
but most of all because they offend Thee, my God, Who art all good and deserving of all my love.
I firmly resolve, with the help of Thy grace,
to confess my sins,
to do penance
and to amend my life.
Amen

And then, because I was beginning to enjoy this, because my body was edging ever closer, I slowed my movements, pulling down the foreskin to expose the glands to the warm air, staring at the precum leaking from the top. "Absolve me, Bishop Jonah," I said pleadingly. "Let me come."

The bishop was close, too. I saw it in his eyes, in the way his lids drooped and that faraway gaze gaining lucidity as the pleasure made him focus

"If I am a holy man, then so, too, is my seed holy. I will spill it on you. Bless your mortal form. Do you want that, Alessandro?" His voice sounded low and heavy and I flushed thinking about his cum, thinking about him spilling it over my face. How degraded I would be—he was my bishop. I had seen him worship so thoroughly, so full of grace. Now, he wanted to come on me—now he was calling it a holy act.

God. And then, correcting myself: *Asmodeus. I want—*

"Yes," I breathed out. "Yes, please, I want it. I want you to—"

He grunted loudly, until the only sounds around us were of our wet panting and the slick noises of our cocks in our hands.

"Close," he muttered, face again contorting, and then he dropped his cane and stumbled forward, left hand wrenching back my head so hard I made an involuntary noise of pain, and something about my expression pushed him over the edge. "God, Holy Father—"

He came in warm stripes onto me. I closed my eyes just as the first splatter of cum hit my cheek. I kept my mouth open and panting like a dog to take his holy water onto my tongue, to take that absolution into me, and in this divine way I came, too.

Shuddering forward, I let myself go in the dirt. Holy ecstasy blinded me, and the bishop was on his knees suddenly, gripping my cheek. I waited for him to say the words that would conclude our confession. *In nomine Patris, et filli et spiritus sancti. . .*I waited for the *Amen*.

He did not give it to me.

"Whore," he spat. And then he laughed, and in laughing the façade stripped away. Bishop Jonah was no longer before me, but some other demonic creature. Distended limbs, skin mottled between red and green hues, and with horns so long and heavy they curled like old toenails, weighted in such a way they pulled and extended the width of its face; it was nothing like Asmodeus. Patchy, thick white hair sprung from its chin and mottled body, and its thin tail whipped at me. Still giggling, the foggy clouds around us parted. I could taste its semen—thick, coagulated—dripping in my mouth, but even that couldn't make me gag. Its cock hung spent and dripping between its legs, thick and ridged.

"Go on, you whore," it cried out. Its voice was scratchy and high, and every word was interspersed with a giggle. "Begin your pilgrimage. Go! Go!"

I rolled in the dust, cheeks flushed with renewed shame. My breeches were still gathered at my legs and I had to shimmy out of them with it staring over me, laughing. I tried to stand, but its tail struck the back of my legs, and I sprawled forward again. Bruises and cuts stung over my knees.

"Crawl," it laughed. "Or you'll never find your way to Asmodeus."

I looked back at it over my shoulder. It watched me with a wild smile, shameless in its lust, and I imagined how I must have looked, cock hanging between my legs, balls rolling over one another with every heavy twist to my hip as each leg scraped over the sand. Helpless and pathetic, just like how Asmodeus had made me. But this creature, wearing the face of an old mentor. . .How could I have fallen for. . .how could I have thought Bishop Jonah was in Hell?

Because he made your life one.

Would I have still done all that for a creature as fetid and ugly as this?

You did do it. You had that cock in your mouth.

I wanted the answer to be no. That I had some line I wouldn't cross. I could excuse losing my sacred virginity to the Prince of Lust, lying about the summoning of Asmodeus, and the murder of Bishop Fazio, but to whore myself out to even a lesser demon? Some putrid creature with no name, and no mention in human texts?

"Bottom of the barrel filth," it called out, like it could read my mind. "That's right. Even *I* had my way with you. What are you now, dear little priest, except meat to be fucked and filled?"

I turned away and started crawling. A heaviness sat in my chest, something close to guilt, and something else: a bloom of private pleasure that was becoming impossible to maintain. Why was I so desperate to hold onto a shred of my dignity, even now, after all that?

The demon whipped forward with its tail and struck against my exposed ass cheeks. That cane-like whack had pain rippling over me, and I arched back with a groan.

"What are you stopping for?" it said. "You have a prince to see. Go on! Hurry!"

It struck me again, and then again when I didn't move quick enough. Rolls of skin bunched at my hips but sweat had made my body slick; the movement lubricated became easier, but it was my knees that held me back. Every motion had grit digging into the skin around the kneecap. After a handful of minutes, a tenderness throbbed in the nerves clustering the bone of my kneecap.

It was then that I finally stopped.

FOUR

I was out of the lesser demon's range—or realm, as I imagined it was. It no longer whipped me, and the fog had moved in a way that once again I had been cut off from everything. Opaque and impenetrable, I could see nothing that would direct me to Asmodeus or my purpose, and instead I had returned to that desolate and solemn loneliness I had first encountered when entering Hell.

In this moment I sat and ruminated. The feelings I had were complex and layered. Shame still drowned me. Every time I thought of Bishop Jonah, I shivered. I couldn't be sure now about any memory I had of him. Had I always been attracted to him? Had the blasphemy and the corruption of an otherwise sexually innocent relationship been the thing to turn me on?

It *was* the blasphemy, wasn't it? I fiddled with my hands and closed my eyes, trying to ignore my nakedness the way Adam and Eve must have tried. In a way, this was my own Genesis. What I was learning of myself now I had never had cause to learn before.

I thought: *if you are this person, who enjoys being degraded, who enjoys being filthy, perhaps you have never been a good person.*

Why that mattered to me, I couldn't say, except that I was still struggling to unite my desire with what I had been taught. The reality of who I was still upset a part of me, even when the rest of me could get off on it.

I sat unmoving and unsure of myself for what felt like hours.

That was, until I heard the singing.

For all that I disliked about the institution of the church, I had been raised in it, and moulded by it, and spent altogether too much time amongst it and its community, to the point where the feelings it could elicit in me were inevitable. I didn't have to be in a gaudy chapel, or some grand cathedral with stained glass iridescent like scales, and incense clogging every corner, to feel God. I didn't have to prayer or take communion or wait for the Holy Spirit to bless me with His voice. When I was younger especially, I could feel him everywhere.

To thieve as a child and be caught, to have my whole life upended with the promise of my self-reform and eternal salvation, meant that in my youthful innocence, I trusted that God was on my side. I thought he had saved me. In those days I could feel Him in the warmth of the sun on my face, or the peace that might settle my anxiety when amongst the other members of the cloth. I found God wherever I looked, because he hadn't failed me yet.

Then the years stretched on and on and what had given me joy once now did nothing for my hollow heart. *He* had no interest in saving the soul of a would-be sodomite. He had no interest in releasing me from decades of torturous suffering; my cross to bear was my devotion to men, my love of the human body, my desire to partake in that pleasure. And the more I thought of what Heaven would look like—a place still so devoid of what I wanted, and instead filled with the love of a God who, by His own standards, could not love me truly—the less I wanted to go there.

You know the rest. You know how I got here. Tell me, then, why hearing that choral hymn ring out in the dry heat of Hell, that I thought:

Return to me, and I will return to you

Malachi 3:7

Return to me. Is that what was happening now? One last ditch attempt at saving my soul, a lifeline in Hell, a promise that if I crawled to Him, He would absolve me of everything I had done?

The singing was amorphous but beautiful. No single voice stood out to me. I sat like a petulant child, naked and warm in that foggy circle, waiting to see if I could understand the trick at play.

Because God would not be here. And if I was honest with myself, I did not want Him here. I had made my own path and I was walking it now.

So, as I crawled towards the sound of the choir, I said aloud: "I am not God's bitch."

Asmodeus in my ear, just a memory, whispered, *"You are mine."*

I crawled through that tunnel with my eyes closed and let the feeling of my righteous betrayal lead me on. Halfway between anxiety and joy, with a touch of rejection; I clenched my jaws and tried to remember what I was doing this for. That I had chosen myself and my own pleasure; that corruption and degeneration of the self suited me far better than piety and eternal, untouched goodness.

What had God ever given me?

Shame! Unrest! Unease of my soul! Guilt that felt

tumorous in my chest and a rabid urge to tear myself apart just to make it all stop!

And the Devil? What had he given me?

Pleasure. An appreciation for my body. A gravity, an anchor for my soul, a reason to become myself.

Like that, with pleasure a mantra in my head, I crawled.

The song was unlike any I had heard, but it had the familiar high-pitched lilt and the serene call of a young voice echoing throughout a church. As I got closer, I could smell incense. Closer still and it choked me with its intensity, but I pushed through, until the wall of fog around me shifted in its consistency. No longer was I surrounded by *fog* but by much incense burning a cloud of haziness around me. I was in a church.

I blinked and in a second the space around me transformed. Rumbling from the ground, columns of stone and marble sprung up in spirals and reached high into the air, dotting the razed earth like giant spears left abandoned after some ancient war. Like a biblical miracle, I bore witness to this great sundering of the earth. Then, from some place beyond the haze, the rest of the church came together. Fragments of stained glass clanked against one another, fusing to form all manner of windows. It was an unfamiliar church, not one I had ever prayed in, and yet homely; it had all the same symbols and trappings of every other holy place I had visited, and by those ideograms, the concept of religion was once again conferred upon me.

My body reacted like I was truly standing in a church of God, naked, with the cum of some lesser demon still staining my mouth. My heart rattled in my chest and nausea flooded me. I cannot describe the intensity of that feeling: of shame and guilt and unnamed fear suddenly pooling in your chest, and no logic or reasoning can do anything to make it go away.

God was in my head with His hands around my throat: *Return to me!*

Return to me, you whore.

God. . . or Asmodeus?

The unknowable voice echoed in the recesses of my mind, but the church itself fell steadily quieter. One by one, voices in that choir were snuffed out, until I could hear only the creaking of chandeliers swaying in the breeze. Where Hell itself was tinted a harsh red, a cold, blue night had fallen over this church. Everything had been cast in an oily blue-black shadow that dripped from every corner.

Shoeless, I crept over the marble. The sounds of my feet—a rounded plap of a footstep—distorted as it echoed, growing sharper on the marble corners of the structure. I felt so small, though not in that delicious way Asmodeus had made me feel. Discomfort ate at me.

Pews upon pews lined the aisle, and I walked down this central vestibule until I met the altar at the end. Old habit came into me and I genuflected, dropping down to give the space respect—which was laughable, given my nudity and everything else about me.

When I stood, I knew my cheeks were flushing from my internal chastising tone. But this upset vanished when I looked up and saw that in those few seconds my gaze was averted, the sanctuary and the altar had changed.

A giant wooden crucifix lay across the altar, large enough for a man to be strapped to. Jesus came to me then, naturally, and I wondered if He would be disappointed in me. In how I turned out.

But He was always the one to save degenerates, some tinny voice cried out inside me.

The issue I faced, of course, was that I still didn't want to be saved.

Still don't want to be saved, still don't want to be saved.

With the same echo of church bells, my own declaration rebounded aloud, as if I had spoken, in this facsimile church.

Something about being here naked at least made me consider what it meant to bear oneself wholly to God. Here was my soul, decked out with the iconography and paraphernalia of my faith, but rotten at its core.

I stepped towards the crucifix. It looked altogether normal, free of nails and blood stains, brand new for its crucifixion. The wood felt rough beneath my skin. I pressed the pads of my fingers into the grooves, waiting for splinters to split them open, or to become jammed beneath my fingernails. Neither thing happened, and when I pulled my hand away, the whole place shuddered.

A cold wind blew through the sanctuary and snuffed out the candles. I spun, expecting company, but no one and nothing appeared before me. Then, in defiance to the wind, the candles reignited—and the light expanded to encompass the whole ruin of the cathedral.

A deep and musical laughter rumbled around me, echoing off the marble and pillars until the sound felt spherical, its origin obscured. I cast about desperate, shivering nude and exhausted.

"Little lamb. . ." a voice cooed to me, and it wafted with the same cloying weight of incense, at once calming and suffocating. My chest relaxed. Minute muscle spasms were put to rest.

"Here you are. . ." called another voice, higher and mellowed, a voice that straddled neutrality.

I waited for the figures to resolve out of the shadows, but nothing changed. There was only me in that windy church. The human part of me was understandably frightened. I hugged at myself, aware of my nakedness the way Adam and Eve had become aware of it; gone was all that joyous pleasure that had come with my nudity, and I was left with guilt and shame once more.

"You seek something," the first voice said.

The second, in answer, "Well, you must seek something, to have risked it all to come here."

I asked, "Who are you?" and my voice shivered, stretched out by the expanse of marble and stained glass, until I could barely recognise my voice in the returning echo.

"Human," one whispered.

"Yes. . . little lamb, that's it. I can smell life in you. Have you opened the door to Hell? Have you let us out?"

The facsimile church bells rang in a clamour, echoing out around the scene. The shadows shifted but still I could see nothing wholly.

I told them, "I opened a door. . .the Cave of the Sibyl."

Some chatter happened then; in a language I couldn't comprehend. I felt it move through me in vibrations. My bones shook with the depth of the sound. But the beings did not share their thoughts with me, and by the time they were done, they had come to some conclusion that moved the conversation on entirely.

Behind me, a shadow shifted, and warm breath tickled up my neck. I flinched and cast about, and once more saw nothing. The disembodied voice said, "I smell something on you. . . someone."

"Asmodeus," I said quickly. My voice sounded like a bark, all defensive. Fear sparked in my gut. "Will you take me to it?"

"Is that what you are after?"

"It must be. The human smells of sex and lust; the prince has corrupted it."

Raucous, hearty laughter.

"I was told to come here. To find it."

"This is part of finding it!"

A growl accompanied these words, and I spooked. I

stepped back until I hit the altar, my hand seeking stability in the wood of the crucifix. Then my arms were wrenched backwards.

I fell with a strangled yelp. In a flurry of movement, and in no more than a handful of seconds, I was dragged up the crucifix by a force I couldn't see. Splinters pricked at my skin and glided easily beneath it, splitting the skin—but I barely felt the pain. The sudden horizontality had me nauseous and distracted. The church became suddenly warmer as braziers shuddered into existence, their heat spreading in comforting waves to every frigid corner, and my body instinctively relaxed even as the crucifix shifted. Grunts sounded around me as the figures moved it, and then—

I screamed.

Nails punctured into my palms to keep me secured to the cross. Instinctively, I threw myself back against the wood, as if fusing myself to the crucifix could somehow relieve me of the pain. As if somehow in this mirroring of Christ's death I might transcend the bloody torture.

But I tell you: it hurt. It hurt in the way that bludgeoned back all pleasure—it hurt primarily, firstly, overbearingly. Even as another part of me can look back at this moment and see the sensuality in it, that version of me was only suffering.

I whimpered loud and writhed, but every movement tugged at the nails tearing through my flesh, and I had to fall limp just to keep new sparking hurt from jolting up my wrists. The demonic presence seemed to enjoy the noises I made, though: appreciative sounds echoed around the church like a hymn. I could smell incense on the unnatural breeze. God, I had been a fool—and yet through it all, my cock twitched with interest.

Shifting, grunting; again, some unseen force lifted the cross, and the burden of gravity slowly encumbered me, until all my weight was pressing at those two nails. If I listened closely, I could hear the tear of tendon in my palm. I kept myself limp, which meant that breathing become difficult and shallow.

"As holy as your lord," one murmured to me when the crucifix had been righted.

I took a shuddering breath, desperate for more oxygen.

"I do not worship him—not anymore!" I shouted, voice cracking with the force. I wanted to be absolved of God's love. I should have been tainted in a way to make these creatures my kind; I had abandoned so much of goodness already. And yet, to have ever worshipped God seemed too large a sin in the eyes of demonkind. I could not shake it.

"We cannot have you lurching your holy body through Asmodeus' realm like this. Still reeking of life and goodness. The church has made its mark upon you; your soul is better than it should be."

"It will not do," the other, higher voice agreed.

"Goodness and piety and shame and guilt—an interconnected sin you will spread like disease should you carry about through its realm."

I didn't understand and, past the pulsing pain in my body, they must have sensed my confusion. Clarifying, the voices said in unison, "You are in Abaddon, little lamb."

Abaddon. An angel of the abyss, or a doom-ridden plane. Revelations says of it:

"They have as king over them the angel of the bottomless pit. His name in Hebrew is Abaddon, and in Greek he is called Apollyon."

But some believed Abaddon was not an angel, but a place.

"Asmodeus rules Abaddon? He is Prince of this realm?"

I couldn't comprehend demonic politics. I was not here to comprehend demonic politics. I was there for debauchery and wickedness and nothing that required much use of my brain. But I required help in finding my master, my prince.

"You misunderstand the point of this place, to think them princes in their own right, and not prisoners," one of the voices tells me.

"But the human has opened a gate."

"I have heard no trumpets. No call to rally. Have you?"

They let the silence stretch so long that I wondered if they expected me to answer. Before I had a chance, they told me, "Asmodeus is not only the Prince of Lust, little lamb. It is also a force of revenge. In Hell, there be nine degrees of demonic legions as contrary to nine orders of angels. And that legion belonging to Asmodeus are named the Revengers of Wickedness."

A term I had never heard of before.

"Is that who you are?" I asked, and they hissed in happy agreement.

"What do you want with me, then?" I whispered. "My revenge on the church and God and everyone in my life is to become Asmodeus' completely."

Again, in unison: "Then let us help you realise that reality, little lamb."

They resolved, then, finally. Two shadows sundered from the umbral dark that hid in the corners of the church and shivered into two distinct forms. The first was so tall its body curved over itself in an insectile posture. It had four arms with gnarled, curled fingers flexing around nothing. Two leathery wings sprang from its back, skin so thin dim light glowed through the translucent flesh. They drooped useless, grazing the back of its hind legs, which had two pivot points like a goat's, but were meaty and thick with hair. Small nubs of horns jutted from its otherwise bald head. The skin stretched taut here, too, seeming as thin as the glassy, vein-infested wings. Both its skin and the furry legs were a wash of dark blue grey, a faded colour with all the vibrancy sapped out of it, which made its yellow eyes hang sullenly in shallow eye sockets. Its mouth was oddly wide and grotesque, and it grinned at me in greeting, splitting half its face apart to bare its jagged yellowed teeth. It had two tongues. Both lolled over its teeth as the creature panted heavily at me.

Its compatriot stood stouter, its form misshapen and gargoyle-like. The face was bulbous, almost a ram's, but with undeniable human features that flung the whole thing into upsetting uncanny territory. It had both horns and tail that reminded me of its master—our master—Asmodeus, though it lacked the Prince's grandeur. The eyes on this creature were feline-like, the pupils pressed thin, and they glowed with the iridescence of a cat at night stalking prey. Beneath its gaze, I shivered, and another part of my body stirred. It assessed me as I assessed it: I took in its muscled form, which made its arms wide and its trunk thick, though its lower ribs pressed through the flesh when it inhaled. Its tail was thick and smooth, without the trident tip Asmodeus' possessed, and the first wicked thought I had was about that thing pulsing inside me. How it might feel wriggling and warm as it worked its way inside.

I flushed, and both demons cackled. The whole church echoed that laughter back, and a confusing deluge of emotion flooded me. Shame and embarrassment, and then the monstrous delight of seeing these demons as they were, their desire plain and devoted.

"Tell me again," I said, for my own benefit. "Tell me what you have to do. Tell me what you mean to accomplish by touching me now."

"We will make you a vessel for his pleasure," the first demon said.

"A wanting, greedy whore."

"God and church and sacrilege and fear still steal your attention."

"Which won't do for our debauched prince," the second assured me.

"If you are to be his toy—"

"—then you must be his completely."

The first, the taller of the two, moved forward. It outstretched an arm—I realised then it had four that I could see—and pressed the sharp nail of its thumb beneath by chin, edging me up to look at its eyes. "But you will have to move through the ranks before you can reach the Prince again."

I shivered and waited for more. Here is what they revealed to me:

That Hell had a complex hierarchy. That they were demons so low they had been given no names. That the lowest named tier were the Presidents of Hell, above which came the Knights, then the Earls, the Marquises, the Princes, the Dukes, and the Kings; and that Asmodeus, though named a Prince of *Lust*, was a King of Hell in his own right. One of nine. They told me that I had not seen Asmodeus in its true form, for I was not yet worthy of it, and that how it had appeared to me on earth was only a shadow of its usual glory and power.

They said that I would need to prove myself to Asmodeus; that it could see all of me and what I experienced as I wandered through its realm. I did not know if they were lying and could not ascertain whether demon loyalty to their Kings was as righteous as I hoped. But in the end, even if they *were* lying, I reasoned that this had been what I wanted.

Sex.

And even if part of my heart longed for Asmodeus, a baser and more feral part of my soul desired anything that would have me.

Snakes hissed and writhed around the pillars, and the braziers burned hotter. Incense clogged the air, reminding me of holy sermon; if I closed my eyes, part of me felt as I had once in amongst my brethren, deep in prayer, waiting for God to touch me. But it wouldn't be God who touched me now.

Two sets of hands pressed upon my skin with an eagerness that had me shivering.

"Open your legs," one commanded, and I did it without thinking. I spread them as best I could whilst hanging from my bloodied palms, feet scrabbling for a foothold in the air and against the splinter-filled crucifix.

Both demons pressed forward and each took a leg, which they pushed high, high into the air, folding me so that my feet were pressed up near my hands, my legs spread wide and my cock and hole exposed. I flushed—and then realised they meant to suspend me there.

"W-wait!"

They did not wait, and two sharp bolts of pain shuddered through me again as they nailed my feet to the wood.

My entire body convulsed. The feeling was confusing. Layers of dread and pain washed over me, and the sparks of sadistic pleasure throbbed beneath them. It hurt. The animal part of brain wanted it to stop. But me, Alessandro, who had done so much already to come here? To have these creatures laughing, slapping at my pale thighs, teasing the underside of my twitching cock with their long-nailed fingers?

That me. . .almost *liked* it.

Sticky blood dripped from my hands and feet and ran down my arms. My breathing became erratic; I looked down at the hungry eyes of the demons, fear and desire both competing for a place in my stomach.

"Hush, little lamb," the taller one said.

The other moved forward silently. "Let us remove the dredges of your faith from you."

I felt God in me, then, the way He had never been. This lingering remnant of the Holy Spirit, now a corruptive force rather than a shield or a protector. Years of teachings and shame of my true nature still clung to me—one good fuck by the Prince of Lust, one measly murder, one giving up of one's old life—none of it was quite enough to dislodge something as insidious as shame.

But at the end of this, whatever *this* was, the pair of these demons promised I would have no regrets.

There was nothing else to be done.

I do not think they needed my consent, and yet they seemed to wait for it. They wanted me to commit to this with honesty and glee. In the end, it was an easy thing to offer.

"Yes," I said, and the three of us shivered as the air in the church shifted. "Yes, make me a creature of lust."

The taller one leaned forward and kissed my neck. Both its tongues slid over my body, and its four hands roamed, teasing at my nipples, pulling at my hair. The other creature reached up and pressed it hands against the cheeks of my ass.

It spread them open.

Spread me open for devouring.

I flinched away, jolting back, but of course there was nowhere to go. It cooed to me, told me to calm; that it would ruin me in due time, but that there were other sensualities I had yet to experience.

It pressed forward into the cleft of my ass with its tongue outstretched. I felt its warm exhale drift over my skin. And then it licked.

I whimpered.

This was—worse. Worse than anything I had experienced. Panic flared in me, and I jolted away from the demons warm tongue, but it pressed hard. My back gave out as I tried to jump away, still folded upwards and impossibly exposed. An ache spasmed through my neck—I couldn't get away.

"Please", I said. "Please stop."

It only laughed. "This is for you. This is your pleasure."

Which it was. And it *did* feel good. But in me there was a

resistance, a disgust, a rejection. I realised I had never fantasised about this kind of lust. In my mind, I had always been had; fucked mercilessly, used for someone else's pleasure. I found it was so much easier to have it taken than to receive it. So much easier to be used and used without mercy. I could conceive of a world where I was nothing but meat to be fucked, a set of holes for cocks to slide in and out of. I could be used until my body gave out and that would make sense to me. I could find pleasure in that degradation.

But for something to try and give *me* pleasure? I had never felt so guilty. I had never felt so—wrong.

My cheeks burned with infernal flame. Both demons moved slowly, the first with its roaming hands, fingers gently circling my nipples, plucking at them, and then slowly sucking, each tongue long enough to reach both simultaneously. The pleasure pulsed down through my body as if everything was interconnected: touching the nipples felt the same as touching my cock. This, combined with the consistent roll of the other's tongue over and into my hole, made me hard in seconds, straining high and leaking precum with such intensity it appeared like I had never touched myself before now. I squeezed my eyes shut like that would be enough to block out the indecency, but two hands pressed against my face and a voice whispered—commanded—"Open."

It sounded like Asmodeus.

I opened my eyes immediately. Reflected in the iris of the taller demon, I saw it; it loomed distended, speaking through the eyeball, in the same form Asmodeus had taken when it had first come to me. I saw it sitting on a throne surrounded by flames, the heat dancing in the eyes of the lesser pawn that debauched me now. I knew an order when I heard it.

I kept my eyes open.

The taller of the demons saw my determination as my expression settled, and it laughed at me, opened mouth and gleeful. "Do not think so highly of yourself," it warned me just as the other one pulled its mouth from me; I felt it leave a slick trail of saliva behind, my hole shamefully wet. Hands pulled my ass apart, long-nailed thumbs digging in with desire. One hand moved and a spit-slick thumb pushed inside. I bucked forward with a groan, and the taller demon's clawed hand latched onto my cheeks.

"Ah—" Pain seared through the meat of my cheeks and my mind went gloriously blank. If I closed my eyes, I was once again being had by Asmodeus.

The demon spat on me. I closed my eyes just as warm saliva spattered over my face.

"You are nothing more than a wet hole and a warm mouth. For us, for a hundred other demons to use—you are our broodmare. A cocksleeve. You are not special to a king of Hell, the Prince of Lust."

I groaned. Halfway between shame and arousal, those words made my cock jump. I locked eyes with the taller, trying to maintain some semblance of composure as its spittle dribbled down my stinging cheeks, and its brethren fucked in and out of me with its thumb. I squirmed and grunted, and wanted to close my eyes—God, how I wanted to look away, to enjoy this without shame

"Say it," the demon growled.

"I am your cocksleeve."

A tail whipped over the underside of my thighs, once, twice, three times. I writhed. Pain—pain sharp and bright and stinging—made me yelp and scream. A confused mix of pleasure and pain collided in my brain as the other's demons thumb kept working in and out of me. It had me squirming. More—that was what I wanted. They called me their cocksleeve but teased me so torturously with only a thumb and the sharp whip of a tail. I wanted them to prove it. I wanted them to split me over their cocks, the pair of them; I wanted to be broken and pathetic and whimpering for more. If they were going to fuck shame out of me, then I needed to forget God. I needed sex to be my religion, an altar I could worship at, or be fucked over, communion the gift of their cocks on my tongue.

I said: "You better ruin me. The both of you—soon. I want—"

A sharp slap to the face. My head lurched to the side and a thin line of drool dripped from my mouth as I bit down hard on my tongue. Neither of them let up, one still finger-fucking me and the other whipping at my red raw flesh. I quivered, whole body tense.

"What you want," one said, their words punctured by the whiplash sounds and my answering whimpers, "does not fucking matter."

I don't recall how long they kept me like that. My body shined with a layer of sweat so thick my back slid against the crucifix as I bucked and rolled my hips. Fingers began to scissor my hole open, and then the way Asmodeus had done, the taller one's tail pushed inside me. At the same time, its dual tongues lapped over my swollen cock.

"A...*fuck*..."

It came out like a sob. I had never experienced pleasure even close to this. On the back of a stinging pain, with demons grinning at my stifled pleas, I felt myself straining against the nails in my feet, urging myself to spread my legs even wider.

With the fingers and the tail moving differently, there was not a single second of reprieve from the rigorous fucking. Both pulled back to look at me, and ordered I look back: "Look at us, filthy priest!" they commanded, and my head lolled down, bouncing between my shoulders as they moved without mercy. My body was hot, and the consistency— scraping against my prostate, fucking ceaselessly—had me coming quickly, pumping into the air.

Bliss.

My head rolled back as I rode out this protracted orgasm, my hole clenching and unclenching around the things pulsing inside my body, until I clenched around nothing. Dizzy from orgasm, I hadn't noticed them both pulling out, until I looked up in time to watch the larger of the two feeding its fat cock into me.

They hadn't opened me up enough.

The pain felt like this: sharp, severe, localised, a little alarm ringing in the cleft of my ass. I strained and jumped away, edging my hips higher into the air, but the four-armed demon hauled me down and kept me in place as the other repositioned itself.

My breathing was erratic and shallow. Fear had laced my desire; I wanted it, and I didn't want it. In a flurry I said, "Wait —! *Wait!*"

Panic overrode pleasure. My spent cock flopped useless and dripping in the air as I fidgeted, but the demons whispered to me.

"Stay still, little lamb," one cooed.

"You wanted this. You begged for it."

"Please," I whispered, meeting the eyes of the one holding me in place.

"See?" The pair of them laughed, and I flushed so hot from their rancour. "There you go again, begging like a bitch in heat."

And those four rough hands became six as the other demon held onto my thighs and pulled me onto its cock.

I didn't open easily. My hole shuddered apart, and I screamed, eyes disappearing in my skull so hard that my vision whited out. I felt nothing but the girth and the warmth, my hole spasming as it adjusted to the sudden size, but the demon didn't wait for me to relax. It started grunting short and fast, ramming deep into my guts, its grip tight around my thighs.

At first it felt sharp, but soon my pleasure doused that pain, and I ground my hips down to meet each thrust.

The other one lifted its four hands from my body and used them instead to tease my nipples and cock at once. Over-stimulation hit me almost immediately. I forgot what I had been concerned about. I forgot to be embarrassed. I let myself get fucked, let the demon's cock slide in and out of my dripping hole, and I rode the pleasure that pulsed in waves up my spine. The demon's cock wept precome into me and with every thrust my hole became looser and wetter. When it tired, the fucking turned slow, but each thrust stayed brutal, balls slapping against my taint and cock scraping deep.

I must have been whining and crying out, for the other one turned my chin towards it and kissed me. Both tongues met mine, and my body dipped into a new state. I felt drunk, my head woozy. I suddenly couldn't see straight, with everything fogging in my periphery, a vignette of pleasure focusing me on the two demons touching every inch of my body.

"Such a cock slut," a voice said, and it echoed back with a choral harmony, near angelic in how it made me feel. Yes, I was a cock slut. Yes, I was desperate, and pathetic, and perhaps I had been born to be used for the pleasure of demons. That was my entire purpose.

"Aren't you?" three light slaps against my face, calling my wandering attention back to them. "Say it, slut."

"I am such a cock slut," I breathed out. "Yes—I. . .I am meant for this. I am meant to be used."

They clicked their tongues at me.

"Pathetic."

"Good boy. You want another cock in you, don't you?"

Part of me winced—no, I can't, *I cannot, I will break*—and this part of me, in its blasphemous manner, almost called out to God for His mercy. But there was no mercy in Hell, no mercy from these creatures, and even if begged for it, I knew I would be betraying the seed of purpose I had unfurling in my stomach. Because it was not a 'want'. It was a craving. A necessity. Lust burning as hot as hellfire—I begged, and my voice sounded foreign, belonging to some other, braver man as I called out, "Fill me. Break me on your cocks."

The whole scene around us sighed. There was a great unfurling, as if there had been a shared tension in all of our bodies, and my plea had popped it open. A rush of warm air swirled through the church in a barrage, and there was a clamour of bells that rang in echoes with great intensity. All thought collapsed beneath the sound. And when the demons leaned forward, their eyes predatory with lust as they kissed me, my mind left my body.

Perhaps it was my soul detaching itself from the flesh. It floated up with my consciousness—the priest monk who had spent decades marinating in his shame—and I let it go. Left behind was the animalistic urge, the pull to pleasure, and an eagerness I could not ignore.

Yes, this was right. I had been cowardly for too long, unable to commit in spirit to what my body had already done. But now, with the shackles loosened, I could slip free. God could not see me here.

Only Asmodeus could.

I flexed my hands and feet against the nails plunged through them. The blood had already crusted around my palms, but the soles of my feet remained sticky and slick. At this angle, my spine twinged in discomfort, and I knew even the most minute of thrusts could be enough to dislodge something significant or could cause great pain. Which frightened me as it would any man—and yet also. . .

I felt both their cocks pressing against my hole, their heads kissing the twitching open thing. United, they pushed forward, and pressed me open.

In some kindness, they moved slowed enough that I did

not lose consciousness. I clung to the blurry vision of their gleeful, delirious faces to ground myself, even as my flesh twitched and stung and rebelled against the press of those too-large lengths. My body fought it, but also loved it—my already spent cock jumped back to life between my legs, slick with precum. I shivered when their hands roamed over my chest, trying to calm the animal response my body had towards the panic and the pain. But as they kissed and slid further in, and as I opened, as my body relaxed around the thick mass of them, my mind—broke.

Not enough to forget who I was. Not enough to forget wholly where I had come from. But enough that, as they impaled me, my head tingled so intensely that I lost all meaning except for this act. And by the time they were all the way inside, cocks twitching and pushing up into my guts, and I was rendered nothing more than a vessel for their pleasure, my mind and body had accepted its fate.

I felt with an almost intrinsic glee that I had been born for this.

I had been made completely immobile. The position they had me in meant I was pathetically exposed. Easy to stretch. Like that, I knew how I must have looked. Pink cheeks, flushed to red. Sweat pooling and dripping down my chest, my hair a ragged mess. With my limbs forced above me, I hung weakly and open. I could offer no resistance; I was a hole to be used without end; I could die here and not impede their pleasure. Fear jolted through me and turned to a corrupted kind of pleasure—I was nothing but a piece of fuck meat, and whether I wanted this or not, they would take me.

They fucked into me. I knew I was warm and wet and tight, opening more and more with every out of sync thrust. They each fucked forward independently, so at every second an entire length of cock was inside me, and every second I had no break, I could barely contain myself.

Both took advantage of the angle, so they could move in me at the same time, and they thrust up *hard*—

"Go—"

Old habit overcame me. I flung my head back, biting off the last of the sacrilege. I would not call to God. Not anymore.

"Hn—"

Pain buckled and gave way to a pleasure so profound, every thrust felt like they were touching the back of my brain. I felt so wholly *had*, so gloriously used, and my body melted into a sexual oblivion.

No more fighting. No more resisting.

I ground my hips back and they laughed up into me.

"That's it."

"Entertain us, little lamb. Show us what you have abandoned your God for."

I could barely do anything but thrust weakly, but I did what I could, groaning and begging. My pleads were little more than incoherent whimpers, the occasional complete *please* slipping through the flurry of incomprehensible moans.

One of the four-armed demon's hands made its way to my mouth. Silently, it urged me to suck on its clawed fingers, but it kept pressing deeper and deeper until I was gagging on its slick digits. Its thumb grabbed the underside of my jaw and held on as it pumped into my ass. I bit down and it made no reaction except to move its hips faster, harder— until I was gurgling a scream into its hand, my eyes lost in the heavens.

"Fuck—fu.."

The church smelled of sex. Like an unholy incense, it spread cloyingly to every corner; the smell of precum, of sweat, of the demonic sulphur and whatever naturally left my body. Condensation fogged the stained-glass windows and the light dimmed. I could see nothing but their panting faces. I was nothing beyond this moment, which stretched out the way my hole stretched, destroyed so completely I could never be anything more than this.

I start to lose consciousness before they were even done milking me. Slipping in and out of this blissed out state, I know they used me for hours, until all resistance was gone and I was broken.

I came suddenly, and more than once, spilling into the air, and later jerking, releasing nothing from the tip. But they had none of a human's limitations.

When they came, the first time, I thought I would burst. I felt the warm splatter inside me, and groaned from that unique pleasure. Only the fluid didn't stop.

I waited, and moaned in waiting, and when still they showed no sign of stopping, I panicked. I flung my head forward, because their come had splattered deeper into me now, and for the first time in my life I could feel something traveling to my stomach from the opposite end.

I squirmed. Panic made me jolt and writhe, and they both laughed and kept me still, even as my stomach began to grow distended, bloating with their cum. Hanging as I was, I could see the definitive rise of swollen belly

"Fucking cow," one said. It cupped my chest, ran a hand over my aching belly, and returned to thumb my nipple, twisting as it spoke. I jolted and moaned. This demon, the shorter of the two, slipped its cock from me slowly. I watched its wet cock flop down between its legs. "You look so good like that, little lamb. So pretty."

The discomfort didn't let up. I rolled my hips over the remaining cock in me. This demon locked me in place with its four hands and grinned, sliding its softening cock in and out a miniscule amount. That motion was enough to slosh the cum in my belly, and I whimpered.

"Pl—please," I whispered, but I didn't even know what I wanted.

"You want release?" the demon above me cooed.

The other moved close to lick at my ear. It sucked on my lobe and opened its breathy mouth to whisper, "How long can you keep our loads inside you?"

I flushed. I didn't know. It was uncomfortable. My skin strained, and stomach ached. But the thought of being forced to hold the semen of demons, to carry loads so large they had deformed my stomach, made my cock twitch once again back to life.

The smaller demon moved to work both its hands up and down my shaft painfully slowly. I gasped and thrust, hole still plugged tight by the other demon's cock. I can't recall how many times I came that day, but it was enough that every stroke of the demon's hands felt at once pleasurable and aching. My poor spent cock came quickly, with only a trickle of translucent cum to show for it, and I was riding that final blissful wave, the taller demon slid itself from my hole with a wet plop.

It wasn't immediate. For seconds my hole twitched and clenched over nothing but air. But then I felt the warm cum leaking out of me. The demons watched, and the church had fallen so silent we could all hear the plap of cum dripping onto stone.

Fuck.

"Push it out," one commanded.

The other gave an answering laugh. "Yes," it said. "We want to see you struggle."

Flushing, but too far gone to feel embarrassed, I listened to the order. My hole twitched. The air felt cold around the entrance, made warm only by the exhales of the demon closest to it and the dribble of cum leaking out. I strained to push out their loads, grunting and aided only by gravity. They watched hungrily, and I had no hope of covering myself. They could see it all with my body exposed like that. I pushed, and cum expelled from my gaping hole. I took breaks, pushing over minutes, and in time my stomach slowly deflated. Sweat dripped into my eyes from the effort. Fuck, it felt like work, and like pleasure, and like something that would have destroyed my younger self; every second that I was displayed like that on the crucifix was further proof of just how precisely ruined I had been. But this version of Alessandro felt a blissful and certain calm, head foggy and mind suspended in a state where I was nothing more than this. And if that was the case, if the creatures here expected nothing more of me than to take their cocks and their cum, then it was Heaven, not Hell, I had wandered into.

Before I was done pushing them out completely, the taller of the two stepped forward with clawed fingers outstretched. It hummed appreciatively at what it saw and played with the cum leaking from me. It pushed it back in, wiggling its fingers over my prostate—to which I yelped—and it stared in fascination at the mix of cum and whatever other bodily fluid of mine had mixed with theirs, scissoring its fingers apart inside me. Then it reached over me and smeared its cum-covered fingers over my glistening chest before it dug back inside me for more. This time, it decided to feed me.

"Taste us," it murmured. "All three of us. Taste your ass and our cum. Taste pleasure."

And I opened my mouth with thanks for the meal I was about to receive. I sucked dutifully on those fingers, tasting the salt of sweat, the tang of their cum, the earthy undertone that must have been my own insides.

"Good boy," it whispered, licking my cheek. "Such a good boy."

I moaned, happy and sated.

They both stepped back from me, and the ruins of the church dissolved back to their desert-shaped nothingness. In this wilderness, I remained suspended on the crucifix. With its tail, the tailer demon leveraged the nails from my extremities, and without ceremony I fell into the waiting mess of cum, saliva, and sand at the base of the cross. Crumpled like that, I lay exhausted and spent, with consciousness fading.

"Well done, my little priest." It was Asmodeus' voice, echoing to me through the voices of the two demons before me. I strained to look, but exhaustion made my lids so heavy I found it difficult to do anything. The scent of cum and sex pervaded my nose. Cum began to dry on my cheek. I thought about sleeping here.

"My pathetic Alessandro, you are not done yet. You have far to go before you prove yourself worthy of being my toy, my pet, my lover in truth. Do you understand, little priest? You will give your hole to any demon you encounter. You will whore yourself out, let yourself be defiled. My realm is lovely, lustful, and deep, and you made an oath to me, a promise you will uphold. So come to me, little whore. Come to me."

The command echoed out around me, prayerful and comforting, and all I could think of, all I could say, was: "Yes."

My journey into Hell began like that. The unnamed demons who made a valiant attempt to rid me of my shame had told me of Abaddon's hierarchy. There were generals and dukes and princes of this plane; demons with bodies I could not conceive of, lying between me and my Asmodeus, Prince of Lust, King of Abaddon. I had not even seen its true form yet, if these two were to be believed. I had so much more pleasure to learn of.

The prospect of so many bodies, so many configurations, so much untapped pleasure stretching out before me—I felt near mad with the possibility.

But there it was. The thing I had been searching for me entire life.

Purpose.

A purpose I could achieve. A purpose that would fulfil me, would satiate me. One I could dedicate myself to with true and happy glee—yes.

With consciousness fading as I lay in the viscous remains of my sex, I remember thinking, "I will come to you, my lord, if it is the last thing I do."

And like that, Alessandro who had once been 'Don', who had once been priest, who had once been God's, now belonged to Hell.

About the Author

Lucien Burr has a background in the Classics and is an author and creator writing dark fantasy stories.

Also by Lucien Burr:

PRINCE OF LUST

THE TERAS TRIALS

 x.com/lucienburr

instagram.com/lucienburr